Pu

The Sigma Menace: Book 5

By Marie Johnston

Pure Claim

Alexandria King's life was ripped away, destroyed by the evil organization Sigma, and one of its most vile leaders, Madame G. Alexandria was imprisoned, tortured, conditioned, and trained to become one of Sigma's finest assassins - Agent X. Except, despite what Sigma ordered, Agent X's only mission became keeping the secret of her bloodline, and using it to destroy Madame G. She's willing to sacrifice everything to carry it out, even her own chance at happiness with her destined mate.

Guardian Commander Rhys Fitzsimmons isn't willing to let the vivacious, frustrating female, who is supposed to be his mate, throw her life away, even for such a noble cause. When her single-minded mission almost destroys her before she can carry out her destiny, he breaks all the rules to save her. But her destiny was not as they were led to believe, and the real threat to their relationship is bigger than either of them could have known.

Thank you Sahara Kelly. Not only do I look forward to the beautiful covers you make, but also your entertaining emails, words of encouragement, and advice.

Chapter One

Madame G must really be pissed.

Agent X swung gently, listening to the incessant drip, drip, drip of her own blood hitting the dank cement floor. A narrow slice into her jugular kept the blood draining slowly out of her upturned body.

X didn't bother to gaze up at her battered form anymore, knowing full well what she'd see—naked, bruised flesh, feet hooked into chains attached to the ceiling with a pulley system. Her arms hung down, fingers touching the cool floor where her blood pooled and congealed, until the next set of Agents came in to teach her a lesson.

X affectionately called this form of punishment the piñata treatment. Beat to hell, stripped down, and strung upside down to bleed out slowly, keeping the subject weak and confused, as they continued generating enough blood to remain alive. She might be weaker, but as Agent… *Dude, which Agent was that? K? H? Ummm… Didn't matter.* He got the shit pounded out of him for trying to take advantage of her tortured state. X would tolerate the abuse until Madame G got her panties out of a wad and decided to put X back on duty. She wouldn't tolerate anyone getting off on her demise.

Unfortunately, X was starting to think her dark mistress kept a real grudge. One where Madame G might decide having indomitable Agent X around wasn't worth wondering if she was playing for Team Sigma or Team Kill Madame G.

How long had she been strung up? Roughly one beating a day, let's see…X counted seventeen beatings, so nearly three weeks of punishment. Three weeks of hanging upside down, waiting for the next beating, enjoying getting hosed off with frigid water so the process could be repeated. Either Madame G forgot about her (doubtful), or she was waiting for a moment that was not in X's best interest.

Normally, subjects were lowered to get a proper kick-and-break-all-your-ribs, take a boot-to-the-face treatment, before getting fed, but X was too risky to lower any longer than to eat a handful of raw hamburger. As Agent S found out—*Yes! I knew I'd remember!*—even hanging by her ankles, bleeding out, she was a force to be reckoned with.

Not for much longer. Being held prisoner for weeks, she hadn't had time to feed, and, oh yeah, there was no one safe to feed from around these parts anymore. Her partner, Agent E, had made his escape to freedom with his wife and kid. He'd been her primary blood source for over ten years since they'd first met.

That day was the end of Alexandria King.

After her life got ripped away by the sadistic bitch who ran this chapter of Sigma, she survived everything the female had put her through. Madame G had wanted her broken, begging to live, begging for it all to stop. X never begged. When E had been thrown into her cell to defile her, doped up on the powerful aphrodisiac that Madame G preferred, something about X had reminded him of his humanity, and he couldn't carry out his task. X had been ravenous and she had ripped out his neck vein and half his shoulder to feed.

When he healed and regained consciousness and discovered her dual species secret, they had formed a solid alliance. X's resistance had earned grudging respect from Madame G, so when X and E offered to partner up and serve Sigma, the dark mistress listened. She decided it would be fun to have a shifter on the payroll, a minion who would be trained to seek her own kind and destroy them.

With E's help, they constantly undermined Madame G's authority. It was like a game, setting their own limits of what the evil bitch could push them to and researching every possible way to get close enough to take her out. E offered his blood to X's vampire half and kept her secret, she covered for him so he could monitor the family he'd been forced to leave behind.

Then Madame G had gotten greedy and put E's family at risk. In order to save them, he had to abandon the plan he and X had staunchly carried out for the last decade. As a nice "in your face" to Madame G, his new chemistry, à la Sigma's Agent enhancements, allowed him to mate his human wife and save his son. Maybe he could've done all that without X's help, but she couldn't have handled failure. Not when it came to E and his family.

God, X missed her partner. She would say he was like a brother to her, but once upon a time, she had a brother, whom she loved very much. Her relationship with E was so much deeper. Not sexual, not like a BFF, but hell, like her other half, a twin.

E was gone, his family needed him more. X had to remain, to continue on with the plan. Her plan was never about revenge. Like E, she had a family, too. A family who could never live freely while Madame G was alive. The madwoman was after a vampire-shifter hybrid, a female, who was reputed to be the Achilles' heel to Madame G's power.

X was that hybrid. Madame G didn't know it. Suck it, G.

Swinging gently, her fingers trailing through her own pool of blood, she didn't feel like much of weapon of Madame destruction. Circling her fingers through the blood, she lifted them up to her mouth, wincing at the pain shooting through her stiff joints, to suckle her own nutrition back into her body.

Gross? Hell yeah. But necessary.

Repeating the process until she wiped up all the blood her wooden fingers could reach, X went back to rocking gently and wondering what all the downtime meant for her future.

Which might be terribly short because she felt a malevolent presence headed her way.

The door drifted open revealing a blood-red kimono-clad tall female with pitch-black hair pulled into a high and tight ponytail. Eyes that could swallow souls landed on X.

X bit back *To what do I owe the honor?* She was treading pretty deep water as it was. Instead, she remained silent, being as respectful as a naked shifter, hanging upside down, covered in blood, could be.

"You've disappointed me, Agent X." The female's ominous tone made X's stomach fill with dread.

Her one goal in life, her *only* goal, had been to wipe this evil female off the face of the earth. Bonus points to destroying everything she had built. X was prepared to die for her mission, had sacrificed nearly everything. It'd be a damn shame if she were killed before she could carry that out.

"My apologies, Madame G."

The dark presence loomed over her. X kept staring at where Madame G's feet would be but were always covered by that damn kimono. She and E had a running bet, whether Madame G wore spiked heels that could impale an eyeball or if she went barefoot. X's money was on sadistic heels, in fuck-me red.

"I'd ask you questions, but I can no longer trust you, so it's a moot point."

Madame G paced in front of her and X strained to get a glimpse at the madam's chosen footwear. Whoever was wrong had to wash the blood and ashes out of the trunk of their work car for two weeks. E wasn't a Sigma lackey anymore and X's keys were no doubt yanked permanently, but she'd hang onto the gloating rights.

Come on spiked heels.

"Seer said she sees you at my back when I rise over the shifters once and for all." The pacing stopped. "So I can't kill you," Madame G spit out. "I want to make you suffer, but you and I both know you've been through everything I have to offer so it'd be a waste of resources." Pride rang in Madame G's voice.

One thing commanded her respect, and it was a person who could tolerate pain and humiliation, yet still have a backbone. No Agent refused Madame G and lived. X had. Plenty of times. There were a few missions where X and E had stood before the madam, their necks bared and ready to lose their heads, because they refused to carry out certain commands like, oh, kidnapping and torturing children. Both X and E had mad field skills and brains in their pretty heads. Neither one was batshit crazy, unlike a lot of Agents, so Madame G made other use of their talents.

Despite their transgressions against Sigma, X and her partner felt the burden of guilt at being nearly powerless as those distasteful, and morally wrong, missions they had refused were carried out by other Agents. Sure, they had done what they could to cause those missions to go awry, unknowingly setting up conditions for the Agents to fail and their prisoners to escape. Then they'd come back to the compound and hear about the innocents other Agents had brought in, who were currently in misery, or meeting their end-of-life requirements. Or there were the interferences that failed. Those weighed heavily on X's heart.

"But Seer didn't say," Madame G continued, daintily squatting down, moving her knees to one side so she could peer into X's eyes with her depthless black orbs, "that you had to be in good condition. Therefore, consider yourself terminated."

Jobless, huh? Madame G continued to drill into X's eyes. Was she expecting an *aww, shucks?*

"You will hang here, X," she hissed, making a point of not addressing her by the title of Agent, "until I dominate the pathetic species of shifters and use their slave-prophesied hides to take over all Sigma chapters. I will use my power to control those ancient, frail male vampires who dare to lead our superior species." Madame G spit in the fresh pool of blood under X's head.

Damn, now she'd have to wait until the next hosing before she could ingest nutrition. No way was she going to take in any more of Madame G than had been put into her when she had been captured.

"Make no mistake, X," Madame seethed, leaning down further, "I *will* dominate. And when I do, I will drag your sorry hide up to rejoice in my celebration."

Reaching a long, blood-red nail down into her splatter of spit, she scraped some off the ground and jabbed her nail into the non-healing wound at X's neck, ensuring that it would stay open and seeping for days. Usually, the Agents had a special pre-made concoction they would use to coat their knives. It would reopen the cut every few days, or a shifter like X would eventually heal themselves. But Madame G's special form of evil exuded from every facet of her being, thus her spit had its own powerful anticoagulant. A vampire whose bite no one could recover from.

Bitch.

Make no mistake Madame G, X mocked in her head, *I will dominate you.*

As Madame G shifted to rise, X peeked under the floor-length garment before it settled back down straightened legs. She caught a flash of a thick, silver post in lieu of a heel and a spike-lined, red leather toe box with her acute vision before the whisper of fabric blanketed them.

In your face, E! X totally won that bet. The dark madam left the room to let X continue to bleed out. X had one other thought beyond destroying the female. *Where the hell did she get those sweet shoes?*

***

"We need to make our move now." *Dickhead.* Commander Rhys Fitzsimmons left that part unspoken. It was certainly implied, and the arrogant prick of a vampire standing in front of him knew it.

"Rhys. Dude," the male tried placating him, "all my people aren't in place yet. If you want this done once and for all, I need time."

The haughty male moved over to be in deeper shade, giving the commander some satisfaction that he was uncomfortable in the dying daylight. But it was the safest time for the male to sneak away from Sigma's compound. He was powerful enough to withstand fading sunlight, especially under the shade of the thick trees in the woods surrounding the Guardians' headquarters.

"She doesn't have time, Demetrius." The male was willing to help Rhys save X, and that was the only thing that kept Rhys from pounding his face in.

Demetrius rolled his pale-green eyes, regarding Rhys as he would a petulant child. "Madame G isn't going to kill her, Commander, just keep her incapacitated for an indeterminate amount of time. I need to get my people in place."

When the aggravating vampire first approached him, all Rhys cared about was how Demetrius could help rescue X. And that was still all he cared about. The vampire's grand plan meant shit to Rhys, other than it would help destroy Madame G, and Rhys could get back to his normal job of policing his

~13~

species. Yes, Demetrius proposed a change so severe that it would rock the vampire world. As far as Rhys' duty went, nothing would change. He would wake up, hunt criminals, keep his species safe, and go to bed.

Only now, he couldn't sleep because there was no vivacious green-eyed hybrid with the funky, glossy black hair that was shaved on the sides. With her longer hair, she constantly styled it in various formats: faux hawk, slicked back, slicked to one side, or hanging over one eye. Her hair had almost as much personality as she did. For years he stalked her dreams, keeping them terror-free so she could get some decent sleep and not be killed the next day.

For almost three weeks, he couldn't find her, no matter the time of day.

As soon as he had laid eyes on her, all those years ago, he knew she was his destined mate. While he was trying to reconcile why, after centuries, he had finally met his mate and she was an evil Sigma Agent, X had nearly gutted him with her wicked silver-lined blade, leaving a nasty scar along his ribs.

That began a long, contentious feud between the two of them, both ignoring the fact that they were meant to be together, meant to be lovers, not fighters. It only took a few skirmishes for Rhys to realize there was more to not only his mate, X, but her partner as well. He gave orders to his shifters that only he was to deal with X; the other Guardians would only defend themselves and others as needed, but in no way try to terminate her. To their credit, they followed his command impeccably. Maybe they even suspected the underlying issue.

Rhys didn't want to wait for this vain dickhead to tell him when he could go and save his mate. "You have intel that says she'll be kept alive?"

"From the evil horse's mouth." Demetrius lifted a heavy shoulder. "I asked her if she was offing my favorite toy. Not that it'd be hard for me to find another shifter willing to give me her potent blood," he finished haughtily.

The rumbles of a growl sounded before Rhys could stop it. He hated being reminded that he was basically talking to his mate's ex-boyfriend. Not that there was anything serious between the two of them, just a little my-body-for-your-information exchange. It didn't mean Demetrius had to act so cavalier about the pleasure of being with her. Rhys only had one physical interaction with her, and it was…it was just…She was pretty damn special.

"Chill, my man. You know it didn't mean anything beyond what we needed it to be. Our relationship, if you can call it that, kept her safe and kept my identity secure. If I had to call someone a friend, it'd be Agent X." Demetrius' mouth twisted in grimace. "Except she told me once she hoped my true mate would be a virgin. What kind of twisted soul wishes that for a vampire like me?"

Rhys nearly smiled in spite of himself. X knew how to get to someone. A vampire like Demetrius either hoped he'd never meet his true mate to live a lothario lifestyle or wanted a provocative seductress who was his match.

"If you don't get your people ready in two days, I'm going to top her virgin comment, and hope that your true mate gets pregnant after your first time together."

Demetrius paled and he physically recoiled. "Commander Fitzsimmons! I thought we were starting a budding bromance here, and then you have to go and say something like that."

Crossing his arms, Rhys ruefully shook his head, not wanting to warm up to the guy. "When you meet your mate, you won't care who she is or isn't, because you'll realize you weren't living before you met her." Demetrius waved Rhys' words off, so he kept going. "And when you realize you made another life with your most cherished, you'll find out how superficial everything else is."

"Wise words. For some other dude. Let's move onto the important stuff."

As Demetrius began a rundown of how to put their plan in place when the time came, Rhys couldn't help but hope he'd be around to witness the full-of-himself male get taken down by the love of his life. Then, if Rhys and X, or Alex as he'd begun thinking of her, were still around, they could kick back, throw in a bag of popcorn, and watch the show.

Chapter Two

Before hearing the click of the door unlock, X sensed the male who was about to enter. Mild surprise fluttered X's eyelids open. Was she dreaming?

Heavily-booted feet silently made their way across the filthy floor until the male settled down in front of her.

She glanced up to meet the serious hazel eyes of her shifter mate and gave a weak, wry smile. "Hey Rhys, how's it hanging?" Grimacing at her attempt to chuckle at her joke, she went for a sigh instead.

"How ya doing, Alex?" His voice was soft and concerned, and she was growing really fond of him calling her Alex. She was too far removed from the innocent eighteen-year-old Alexandria King that had been brought here.

He looked like he wanted to touch her, caress her bare skin, but was worried it would cause more pain. He wouldn't be wrong.

"Oh, you know. Just been hanging around." Her voice was raspy, parched from lack of water.

She was only given enough nourishment to keep her alive.

"I'm going to get you down."

She tried shaking her head, but it made her head pound and blood trickle out faster. "You know I'm not leaving here until my job is done."

Caressing her cheek with a work-roughened fingertip, he stopped her argument. "We'll get to that once we get you down and fed. And armed. Then we'll wrap your business up or die trying."

Interesting. *And this totally isn't a dream.* "Howdya get into the compound?"

Irritation flitted across his face. "I had help from a surprising source. It seems there have been others planning a coup."

A lazy grin drifted across X's face. "Big D?"

When Rhys' nodded, her spirits lifted. Maybe they could actually make this happen. She knew Demetrius had been up to something, coming to co-lead Freemont's Sigma chapter. The Vampire Council had sent him, worried Madame G was putting their species at risk with her insane experiments and the way she began turning so many of her recruits into Agents without proper conditioning.

Demetrius had arrived with his cock-of-the-walk swagger and blew off his duties, letting Madame G continue with free rein. Suspecting he also had plans that went against Sigma, X had formed an unusual alliance with the vampire, and he'd helped her and E undermine Madame G's plans.

She had also suspected he had been lacing the compound with his own vampire Agents, ones that weren't loyal to Madame G, or Sigma. That had to be true, otherwise Rhys wouldn't be getting her very far.

"Ready for this?" He waited for her response before trying to get her down.

"Let's do it."

Joints that had been stretched for three weeks, a body that hadn't been allowed to heal, and a head that had been blood-logged from hanging upside down all that time—it would hurt. So bad. Even more than when they dropped her, sprayed her off, and strung her up again.

He rose to standing and moved to her side. He wouldn't have to reach up far to unhook her ankles since he was a tall male. She was nearly six feet tall, but he was half a head taller than she was and wearing his shitkickers.

She caught his scent when he moved. He smelled divine. Like a pine forest. She probably smelled like a slaughterhouse floor. Yes, they hosed her off every day or two, but really, she stank.

His large, hot hand settled between her shoulder blades, and her eyelids actually drifted shut in bliss. No contact for weeks except for boots and fists. It was glorious. Until he started raising her body to cradle her upper half in one arm and undo her bindings with the other.

Nausea hit strong and hard, along with invisible forces slamming into her skull. Against her will, she groaned.

"I'm sorry." He sounded sincere, regretful.

"Not your fault," she tried to murmur, but it came out more like, "mayoufau."

Oh hell, her head fucking hurt and the cut at the side of her neck wasn't helping. The movement was making it ooze even more blood, not that she had a lot left to spare. It wasn't getting heavily persuaded out of her body by gravity anymore, but she could feel the effort of her body trying to heal the Madame G-inflicted wound.

There was nothing in her belly to vomit up, and the commander's hard body holding her was pure pleasure. To ease her pounding head, she turned her face into his shoulder, letting his heat sink in. She was extremely glad he was clad in head-to-toe black because any other color would be hell on her sensitive eyes.

"Two of Demetrius' vampires just came on for your guard duty. As long as no one bothers them, they'll guard us." Rhys had to pause while he grunted and worked the lock at X's ankles. "So," she heard a clang of metal, but her ankles remained firmly bound, "we'll go next door so you can clean up and feed."

If she had any saliva left, her mouth would water. She had only fed from Rhys once before, and due to her hybrid genetics, from now on it would have to be him. Some vampires developed an aversion to blood not from their true mate after meeting them. The thought of other's blood turned her stomach. He was the true mate to her vampire half.

"The hell?" He shifted her to hold her more firmly as he beat on the lock at her ankles. "It's rusted."

The angle he was trying to open it from, while cradling her upper body, couldn't be helping, either. She was about to suggest he hang her back down so he could use both hands, when her legs swung free.

Rhys smoothly caught her under her knees. He remained still, while she stiffened and winced against the sudden movement in her muscles. Her feet were cold and numb, and she didn't have a lot of blood left to rush into limbs that had been strung high above her head. All in all, the lower half of her body didn't hurt nearly as bad as her upper half.

When she settled into him, he strode toward the door and gave it two soft taps. The heavy metal swung out. Agent R was waiting on the other side. He gave Rhys a nod. He looked X in the eyes and jutted his chin up. She narrowed her eyes on him as understanding dawned. Dude had balls.

Agent R—she wouldn't have guessed he would be under Demetrius; he had played his part well for Sigma. He and two female vampire Agents had tracked E and his family down deep in the woods and captured them. They brought him in, but somehow hadn't mentioned the female shifter they had also tranqed, but didn't bring in along with E and his family.

Now it made sense. Demetrius had used Irina Bellamy to get Rhys to listen to him. If she had been brought in, it would've been nearly impossible for the Guardians to rescue both Irina and E's family. X would've been compromised and killed if she had tried to help the shifter escape. Not even Madame G could fault her for helping her partner. Well, not any more than she had. Helping Irina would have pushed her luck too far with the madam.

Rhys carried her down the hall to a locker room used by the guards. On the way, she sensed Agent Z. Or Zitch, as X called her, replacing the "b" because the Agent was one. X liked her.

Zitch had been involved in her punishment, along with Agent R. They had only done their job and nothing more, unlike the other Agents who tried to fuck with her. X could respect that, even as she felt the echoes of their booted feet assailing her body. She'd been in the same situation before, forced to dole out punishment she really didn't care to perform.

Rhys entered the locker room, locking the door behind them. X raised her head, grateful the commander had left the lights off. Weeks spent upside down in a dark room meant her eyes were hypersensitive.

A shower. Nice.

X held onto Rhys' broad shoulders and lowered her legs down to the floor. He adjusted his hold to around her waist, while she gingerly put weight on her numb feet. His hot hands were like brands against her skin.

"Want to shower before you feed?" He spoke quietly, intimately.

She nodded, knowing he could see well in the dark.

He helped her to the shower, keeping an arm around her waist the whole time, while she stutter-stepped on her sore, rubbery legs. Standing to the side of the showerhead, he fiddled with the knobs until a nice, warm spray rained down.

She was about to dismiss him, not wanting an audience for cleaning the blood and grime off her skin, when he said, "I'll get a towel. The Agents put your gear on the bench."

X didn't bother to nod, raising her face to the spray. Maybe they would get discovered at any moment, maybe the Agents would turn on them, but she didn't care. X let the water run over her until she felt revived enough to wash herself. Heaven must feel like a warm shower.

The shower was stocked with everything she needed. *Apology accepted.* Agents R and Z must've banked on how this would drain some of her irritation at their beatings. Totally right. She'd still break a bone or two for payback, but she wouldn't mangle them.

There was even a razor. X felt the sides of her head. Her hair had grown during her punishment, but she'd pass on shaving the sides back down. Once she was done with Sigma, she might even grow them out entirely. After the shower, she would braid the rest of her hair. Nothing was going to get in the way of destroying Madame G.

She shut off the glorious water and chose a towel hanging by the shower entrance. After drying her hair and body, she wrapped the towel around her torso before returning to the locker room.

She was weak, dizzy. It was only partially due to the potent male waiting for her. She was low on blood. The wound at her neck trickled blood, leaving a trail down her chest, soaking into the towel.

"Will that heal when you feed?" Rhys' voice was rough.

She could sense his arousal filling the room. Hers was probably doing the same, but she had no intention of doing anything about it. Not here.

"Probably," she answered.

"Do you want to get dressed first?" he asked gruffly.

No, she wanted to stay naked around him and enjoy the torment of his desire. However, she experienced the same torment and now wasn't the time. "Yes, I'd better."

"You can rest, too, after you feed." X raised an eyebrow at him, gathering her stuff. He continued with an explanation. "We thought if we could pull this off and get you up to strength, we might be able to hunt her down."

"Take her by surprise." X shrugged into her shirt and stepped into her pants, then kept the towel at her neck to catch the trickle of blood.

Rhys didn't say anything in reply. He was watching her every move, his eyes travelling over her body. She was doing nothing more than getting dressed, but from his rapt expression, one would think she was putting on a high-end strip tease. Even once she was fully clothed and had her aching feet stuffed into boots, he still wore the same expression.

"Been a while since you've seen a naked female, Rhys?" she asked wryly.

"Yes. But no one naked can compare to you, even with clothes on."

Awww. She smirked, but it held a hint of shyness. He might actually make her feel all girly.

"You're pretty hot, too." Romantic words and poetry were not her forte. She gave him an impish grin. "For a redhead."

He scowled at her and she almost laughed. He was extra haw on the *hawt* scale. Deep strawberry-blond hair, with a strong face and a ruddy complexion that only complemented a body honed in nature. In human terms, he was a man's man.

"But, I wouldn't know if you're a true redhead. I haven't gotten to see *you* naked," she teased. What the hell she was doing playing with fire? This was not the time to get frisky.

His intense hazel eyes blazed, the green in them almost glowing. He knew she was teasing, but he wanted her. So. Bad. It was a heady experience for a girl.

"Anytime, Alex."

Her breath hitched at the challenge in his voice. Damn, he barely had to do anything to get to her.

To distract herself, she checked her weapons. She wouldn't fully trust Agent R or Agent Z. They had their best interests in mind, X had hers.

"When I feed—"

"I know," he interrupted. "Now's not how I want our first time together to be, either."

He was partially telling the truth. She could sense it. He wanted her, whenever he could get her. But he would respect her wishes and with her fucked-up past, she didn't want to feel anything like Agent X when she was with Rhys. *If* she ever got to be with Rhys. She dedicated her life to eradicating the world of Madame G, and she was still prepared to give it.

He was such a good male. He would have totally been worthy of Alexandria King. X was quite the goody two-shoes before Madame G had gotten a hold of her. Good grades, humanitarian projects, healthy living. She'd had a family who loved her, cherished her, protected her. Now she was Agent X, a stone-cold murderer who used her mind and body any way necessary.

"Alex?" Rhys asked, reading into her silence.

Maybe someday, she thought at the use of his nickname for her. Ironically, it was the name she used when she needed to blend in with the humans. For now, she needed to be X.

"Time to eat," she announced.

"All right, but…" He stalled, clearing his throat. "Can you take my neck?"

X's eyes shot to his thick jugular, and she swallowed hard. When she had fed from him before, it was from his wrist, and that had been an intensely erotic experience. She couldn't imagine the impact it would have with her body pressed into him. Her better judgment told her to say no, they couldn't risk that level of intimacy. Then again, they could both die once they left this room.

Her heart constricted. What if *he* died and *she* didn't? She was prepared to give her life, but what if she was left alive and alone?

It was what she deserved, another part of her brain filled in. She'd been part of an evil organization for a decade. She continued being Agent X even after she knew Rhys was her mate. Did she really deserve the male in front of her?

Fuck it. She'd take his neck, breathe in his scent, drink his blood down, and think about it all later.

She finished inspecting her gear and holstered her last weapon. It didn't look like anything had been tampered with. Then she rose and spun so she was straddling Rhys' lap. His eyes instantly went heavy-lidded as he slid back on the bench and rolled his head to one side.

X's fangs throbbed, and not just from malnourishment. Being this close to Rhys, his throat bared for her, made the most exquisite desire course through her. Ever so slowly, enjoying the moment, she dropped her head down until her lips were at his nape.

He tensed, his hands tightening around her waist. He was resisting pulling her closer. It was like he was almost afraid to breathe, afraid she'd back off and grab his wrist instead.

That would be the smart thing to do.

Flicking her tongue out to lick at his warm, salty skin, she reveled in his groan. When her poor fangs couldn't take any more, she sunk them slowly into his flesh, knowing the burn would feel nothing short of erotic for the male.

His groan deepened, and his hips thrust underneath her. Her mouth filled with rich, potent shifter blood. If her eyes were open, they would've rolled back in her head. Her starved body grabbed up the nutrition, while her core went up in flames.

A whimper escaped and she unintentionally ground down onto Rhys, feeling the hard mass of him trapped by his pants. He pulled her in close as she sank fully onto him. If she hadn't dressed before she bit him, his fly would be undone and she would be fully impaled already.

He rocked his hips up into her and she rode him, seeking the release her body wanted so badly.

The wound in her neck burned as it healed, standing no chance against Rhys' blood. Power surged through her body, desire swamped it.

She rode him faster, preparing for her first fully-clothed orgasm. His arms were wrapped around her, one hand holding her head to his throat. An earthquake started in her center, rippling out in the tidal wave of climax. She shook in Rhys' embrace, crying out into him.

When the tremors passed, her fangs retracted before she took too much from him. Her eyes fluttered open, but not very far.

She was exhausted. Bone weary, her body spent from healing, basking in an orgasmic afterglow, the first she actually enjoyed. Usually, after she got off, it was back to business as usual. Rhys' comforting warmth kept her in place.

"Rest," he said softly.

Yes. Rest. X turned her head onto his shoulder and fell fast asleep.

Chapter Three

He could let her sleep for another half hour and then they had to get going.

Rhys glanced down at X where he had stretched her out on the bench. Even asleep, she exuded power and sexuality. Her ebony hair was now dry and swept back from her face; he could get lost in her creamy complexion that had a natural blush along the cheekbones.

She was intoxicating. And lethal.

And not yet his.

Rhys sighed and leaned back. His erection had finally backed off, allowing him a level of comfort. He'd never been as turned on as he had when she had climaxed with her fangs inside of him. As if drinking from him wasn't erotic enough.

Rhys moved off that subject before his pants became too constricting again. He could tell right away when she came out of the shower she was apprehensive about having sex with him. He wondered if she had ever had sex because she wanted to, or if it had always been forced on her, or used as negotiation. He would wait as long as she needed him to.

Instead, he thought about how heady it was to actually be able to hold her while she was sleeping. Not dream hold her, but as X would say, "for realsies." It wasn't until the first twitch of a nightmare that he shifted her to stretch out, using his dream walking abilities to murmur in her ear. She settled into a healing rest and he had kept watch over her for a few hours.

He was about to check his watch when her vibrant green eyes opened and she sat up.

"Tell me the plan while I put a braid in this mess." X finger-combed her hair to get it straightened out.

Damn, she was good. Even *he* thought she was fast asleep. Life with Sigma had seriously honed her survival skills.

"Shift ends in forty-five minutes. Bennett has the Guardians surrounding the place. When Demetrius gives the signal, his vampires will take care of the Agents and recruits, while you and I hunt for Madame G."

"So that's been his thing all along? Taking out Madame G?" X's fingers deftly braided her short hair tightly to her scalp.

"Even bigger."

She arched a brow. "Sigma?"

"Bingo. The new generation of vampires don't think their council regulates Sigma well enough.

They think the organization threatens their existence and want to see it destroyed."

X whistled low. She finished her braid and tucked it back up into itself since she didn't have anything to secure it with. "That could cause a vampire civil war."

"Yep." He frowned despite himself.

"What?"

"Sometimes I wonder if shifters won't be facing the same thing." She waited for him to elaborate. "Before your partner killed Mason, he said some revealing things to Dani." Dani Santini was the human mate of one of his Guardians. A member of his own pack had almost killed her, but Agent E shot his heart out. Literally.

X wrinkled her nose. "He was always a douche."

Rhys had to agree. E solved the problem that had plagued Rhys about what he was going to do with the human-hating shifter.

"He alluded to the Lycan Council being behind attacks on human mates. Then Madame G hinted that the council was also behind the slaughter of Mercury's village."

X did one more final check of her weapons. The hybrid couldn't sit still, and he was content to watch. "Why would they do that?"

"She posed the hypothetical question of what if the council killed a colony of shifters with uniquely powerful abilities so none of them would fall into

Sigma's hands? Or was it because they thought they couldn't control them?"

"Sounds like you and Demetrius have some major council issues."

"They're your councils, too," Rhys grimly pointed out.

X gave an indelicate snort. "No they're not."

He decided not to argue. It was exactly as he expected. X only allowed herself to be forced into Sigma service so she could destroy Madame G. From what E said, Madame G had tried to break X for almost two years before he came along and they teamed up. She was eighteen when she was captured, and not even sadistic Madame G could destroy her. She was raised to be strong, following no one. There was no way she would submit to either council just because she was the first known vampire-shifter hybrid. And both councils would demand dominion over her.

"Ready." X fluidly rose. Rhys loved watching her strong body move. She was a work of art.

He, too, rose. As much as he wanted to snatch her up for one last kiss, or rather, their first kiss, it wasn't the right time. She was amped, ready to hunt and fight. He was too, but for a far different reason after her feeding.

Rhys went to the door, giving the same two knocks as he had before. Two knocks echoed in return farther down the hall, so he opened the door.

Agent R and Agent Z waited for them. R was only a couple of inches taller than X, with ink-black hair, light-brown eyes, and an olive complexion. He was always partnered up with Agent Z, and sometimes they were partnered with another female vampire, Agent O. Agent Z wore a perma-sneer and kept her long walnut-colored hair drawn back in a severe bun.

"The only way up to Madame G's suite is by elevator," Agent Z briefed them. "We can't even flash up there. Not that it'd do you two any good," she finished with a smug grin about her vampire ability over shifters.

Rhys repressed a smirk. It might not do him any good, but X was a different story.

X made a theatrical show of rolling her eyes. "Ouch, that one hurt, Zitch. Tell me again, how was your last daylight stroll? Oh yeah, you can't even step out the door half the day."

Zitch sucked in on her teeth before shooting back. "Maybe if it's raining. Smelling like wet dog isn't an issue for us."

Rhys remained impassive, but X was never one to let a challenge go. "The last time I smelled wet dog, yo' mama was panting under one."

Zitch's eyes went wide before she broke out in a grin. "Nice. I'll have to use it on Agent O."

Agent R shook his head before turning, expecting them to follow. "Demetrius should be in place."

Getting shot at, I hope. Rhys didn't want to like Demetrius. Aside from his history with X, Demetrius was also cocky and a vampire. If the male was dishonorable and undependable, and didn't care so deeply about his species' future, it would be easier to hate him.

They swept through the punishment ward in the compound, making their way to the creepy stairwell to get above ground. The plan was for the Guardians to attack the facility and engage the Agents, distracting them so Demetrius and his team could wipe out as many as they could.

The structure still hadn't been fully rebuilt since the Guardians launched the assault that helped E escape. Normally, they didn't keep ammo of that scale on hand, but Demetrius had sources who supplied them with heavy artillery, then and now. As far as Madame G was concerned, the shifters regrouped and attacked before she could fortify her headquarters against another attack. They didn't want her to figure out it was an inside job until it was too late.

***

X didn't know how Demetrius and Rhys planned to lure Madame G out of her suite. She rarely left, and when she did, it was only to flash in and out somewhere mysterious. The dark mistress made it hard to get to her for a very good reason. A lot of people wanted her dead.

The elevator would only work if she was expecting someone and wanted them up there. The madam kept her quarters heavily warded so it was impossible to flash in.

Or was it?

Of course, X had never tried. Nothing would say, "Hey, I'm part vampire," faster than a flash. The vampires who worked for Sigma had commented on it, but had any of them ever really tried?

"How does Big D plan to get Madame G out of her hole?" X stopped, causing the rest to do the same.

Agent R answered, "His best plan is to attack and fight our way toward her. She won't leave and let all of her work get taken over."

"We should try to flash there," X replied.

"You on crack?" Z laughed. "Everyone knows we can't flash into her office."

"Have you ever tried?"

R and Z both looked at each other. "Well, no, but we'd have to bring you two dogs with, and the trip would disorient you too badly."

"I've flashed along plenty of times," X lied smoothly. "I'm used to it."

"I'll manage," Rhys added firmly.

X held out her hand. "Hang onto us and you two try to flash past her barrier simultaneously."

Agent R radioed Demetrius. She grabbed onto Rhys' hand, making sure he didn't get left behind if the flash worked.

"All right," R finally growled, showing his fangs. "He's going to signal the attack. Once it begins, we'll *try* to get into her office and hunt the bitch down."

Deep in the recesses of the edifice, they couldn't feel much but faint vibrations as artillery hit the walls. The same walls that were still weakened from the Guardians' last attack. Loaded with even more lead, this time the structure may not survive. Even if they didn't get Madame G, they would seriously incapacitate her for a long amount of time.

Z threw her hand on top of X's and Rhys' hands, waiting for R so they could flash.

By now, shouts filtered through the walls and down the hallway as Agents and recruits were running up to defend the building.

R used both his hands to cup the hands of the group. "One, two, three."

R and Z focused, X watched intently.

Their first attempt didn't work, whether it was due to Madame G's shields or the added weight of trying to bring along two bodies. Both Agents closed their eyes for deeper concentration, and X took the opportunity to use her flashing ability to enhance their power.

They shimmered and disappeared. Instead of instantly reappearing in the deep-red and royal-purple chambers of Madame G, the group hovered in nothingness. It was like they were pushing against an invisible wall, until the flood of potent vampire power overwhelmed even Madame G's cryptic forces.

The abrupt arrival in Madame G's office made them all stumble backward, releasing their hold on each other.

Rhys staggered a little more than the rest, his head shaking, weaving on his feet. For a non-vampire, flashes could be like riding the merry-go-round for an hour; the world doesn't quit spinning.

R and Z wore puzzled expressions. X acted as if she was clearing her head, too.

Rhys, hands outward to steady himself, moved slower. X took the opportunity to scan around. No malevolent force was storming out of any hidden nook or cranny.

They all spun toward a wall at the sound of a strangled cry and Madame G's yell. "Another attack you didn't see?"

"The seer is behind this panel." X rushed to it and hit the lever she saw Madame G use the last time she was in the office.

The panel swung open with a whoosh. Madame G displayed rare emotion on her porcelain face. Shock at the appearance of guests in her office, along with a heavy amount of rage, twisted her mouth and a deadly light shone in her black eyes.

The enraged mistress had a firm hold on the seer's chin. The seer herself had a calm demeanor. Her eyes shimmered with fright and…resignation. The female thought she was going to die today.

Since she was a seer, she was probably right.

Madame G glared at X and the rest of the group, before turning her churning gaze back to the seer. "You pathetic creature. You thought you could deceive me?"

She raised her other hand, her fingernails curled into claws. X and Rhys both drew their guns, but weren't fast enough. Madame G brutally raked her hand across the seer's throat. X had seen a lot of carnage in her life, but Madame G nearly beheading the seer with one hand was among the worst.

She and Rhys opened fire at the madam, advancing on her.

The two Agents flashed to Madame G, forcing X and Rhys to cease-fire so they wouldn't injure the vampires. They needed everyone at full strength.

Madame G snarled at Agent R as he appeared in front of her, while Agent Z popped up behind. Her eyes glowing with rage, Madame G threw a hand up and flung them both backward like rag dolls.

X dodged Agent R's flying body, and just as Madame G's eyes lost focus to flash, she dropped her gun and dived to catch a handful of the madam's kimono.

Everything went black and then X was on grass. Gunfire popped between the trees that surrounded the compound and the Agents trying to defend it. Lifeless bodies scattered close to the building. None of them were Guardians. A large explosion shook one of the exterior walls.

Madame G above her chanted in a language X didn't recognize. A supernatural storm brewed, the wind raged. The fight raging on around them had paused with the appearance of the dark vampire, X attached via death grip to the madam's robe.

Rhys, try to save the seer. We're in the courtyard. X hoped the seer wasn't dead. She wanted answers, dammit.

In the small amount of time it took X to send the thought, Madame G noticed her. Another flash of shock in her dark eyes gave X enough time to roll quickly to the side to avoid getting stomped on by the deadly heels the madam wore.

Sucking in a huge breath as she jumped to her feet, she unsheathed a knife. If Madame G had time to call on the dark forces that had been aiding her, all would be lost.

Unseen pressure squeezed her lungs, she knew Madame G was trying to suffocate her. That might work in her office when X had no other choice but to remain compliant, but today X would not be stopped. Either Madame G or X, or both, would be dead shortly.

X whipped her knife at the madam, who spun to avoid the cut of the blade. The bullet wounds Madame G had received after nearly decapitating the seer slowed her reflexes. X drew another blade in her left hand and charged the madam before her breath ran out.

Instead of stabbing her, X pulled her right arm back and let a jab fly so fast and hard, the crack of Madam G's cheekbone was almost worth the three weeks of torture.

The pressure on her chest released, and X heaved a mighty breath.

Madame G stumbled back, her hands cupping her face. Knowing she was no fighting match for X, Madame G sneered at her before lifting her hands high above her head. Then she flashed.

Fuck!

At the edge of the tree line, facing the compound, Madame G reappeared, her chanting increasing in volume and power. The wind buffeted and a flash of lightening raced toward the area of the compound that held Madame G's suite.

A bolt that was strong enough to demolish the entire wing appeared to hit an invisible dome. X scanned the tree line until she saw Mercury a few hundred yards away with his hands raised, silver gleaming strongly through his features, while one of the twins protected him.

X smiled grimly. Madam G had gotten arrogant, increasing only her power, thinking all other creatures were below her strength. Where she had to sell or barter her soul for more power, Mercury's abilities originated from within.

With her smile in place, X faced Madame G, who was glaring incredulously at Mercury. Then her dark eyes caught X's, and her rage returned. Madame G threw her arms even higher, wind swirled around her skirts, and her entire body lifted off the ground from her power.

That crafty seer. Madame G was indeed ascending over the shifters, but it wasn't going to be the way she hoped. X's smile widened further, and she flashed.

Reappearing behind Madame G, she grabbed the evil bitch in a headlock and dragged her down to the ground, hissing. "It was me you've been looking for all along."

Madame G stiffened as X's words sunk in. X shoved her knife deep into the female's ribs, angling it up. The madam gasped and lightening hit the ground by X's feet.

She withdrew her knife and slammed Madame G onto her back, then straddled on top of her. The air was once again devoid of oxygen, and X jerked as she tried to take a breath. Madame G took advantage and hit the knife out of her hand.

X launched a fist into the madam's face. The hit was enough to stall Madame G's control and allow X to draw a breath. She pulled another knife out of her boot and peered straight into Madame G's evil black eyes. Her look of incredulous shock was deeply satisfying to X.

"You couldn't break me because I was meant to destroy you." With one hand, X grabbed the madam's chin, narrowly missing the madwoman's fangs.

Madame G snarled in fury, her black eyes flashing a rage filled red. Using her knife, X slashed across Madame G's throat and kept sawing the vampire's head off and end her for good.

The wind died down further with each cut, the storm was growing weaker, but X sensed energy building, gathering under her. She gritted her teeth. She had to finish this before Madame G gathered her dark power one last time.

With a final hack, the spinal column severed. Before X could breathe a sigh of relief or celebrate her victory, the energy in the madam's body coalesced and blew outward with a mighty roar.

A flash of light and Madame G's body exploded. X was thrown backward, the air knocked out of her, pain shooting through her jarred bones as she rolled. The percussion deafened her, white light blinded her, heat seared her skin. An inky pit formed under the remains of Madame G and spread to gobble up every speck of the madam's body. X scrambled further back, not knowing what the pit was, but suspecting it had to do with whatever evil forces Madame G dabbled in. X's limbs were sluggish when she tried to scoot herself out of the way. She was bleeding profusely, her ears were ringing, and her head was pounding.

Part of Madame G's arm lay at X's feet. She had to move or the black hole was going to swallow her, too. Her vision doubled, she tried to shake it off. She thought someone was calling her name, but everything was muted.

So this was how it was going to go. X knew she probably wouldn't survive the ultimate confrontation with Madame G, but she didn't think she'd be so helpless. She felt like a newborn kitten that hadn't yet learned to walk and had been drop-kicked down a flight of stairs.

Dimly, she was aware of more shouting, but her consciousness faded and all she could do was watch the fathomless hole creep toward her.

Strong arms secured her under the shoulders. She registered the scent of her mate. Didn't the seer make it, or did Rhys ignore her and rush out there instead? The jarring movement of him pulling her back sent waves of pain through her torn body. Darkness finally claimed her.

Chapter Four

X woke up to muted sunlight streaming through the windows of a small cabin. Shit, she hated passing out and waking up somewhere else.

Drawing in a deep inhale, she sat up and looked around. This must be Rhys' place. She had seen the lodge that housed the main Guardians' headquarters before and the quaint cabins that dotted the woods around it, but she'd never been in any of them. She could've breached their security and spiritual measures at any time but never revealed that info.

Voices murmured out on the porch. No doubt, Rhys was keeping everyone away while she healed. The sonic boom Madame G created when X beheaded her was pretty damn epic. It almost shattered X's body along with it. If she hadn't fed from Rhys that day, she might not have withstood the explosion. Without Rhys to pull her away from the evil black hole that came to claim Madame G, she would've been sucked in, too.

As if her thoughts conjured him, she recognized the swagger of his footsteps as Rhys entered the cabin. He peeked his head in the bedroom to check on her.

She must look like a hot mess. The longer part of her hair was tangled like an eagle's nest swirled high on her head, and she had G-splatter all over her clothes. Rhys was considerate enough not to change her while she was passed out. He knew about the unpleasantness many experienced while unconscious at the Sigma compound.

Instead, he had stretched her over a top sheet in her torn, sooty clothing. She scanned herself. Most of her gear survived. A few hours of cleaning with a Q-tip and it might not stink like blown-up-bitch anymore.

"Hey," Rhys greeted her. "E was here checking on you. Actually, he hasn't left, been a pain in the ass since we got back."

The corner of her mouth quirk up. It'd be good to talk to him. She had missed him, been happy for him, but never expected to be able to just hang out with him again.

Her irritated mate ran a hand through his short hair. "I told them all to wait until you're ready."

She arched an eyebrow. *All?*

He nodded, exasperated that there was so much attention on his cabin. "There's E, and then Ana wants to meet you. At least she has the sense not to be so damn pushy. Of course, your niece and nephew want to see you. Ronnie's all casual, but Sarah's like a yapping Chihuahua." He gave his head a shake. "Dani's been by, too, but Dante's keeping her pretty busy."

Dani Santini. X had been pretty damn relieved when that girl's situation rolled out well. A few mental pushes and a pregnant Dani busted her way out of Sigma and ran into the arms of Mercury. Their bond overrode the one Madame G had tried to create with the baby when she impregnated her with Mercury's semen. Dani and Mercury were happily mated and raising their baby.

X had a role in the lives of many of the humans and shifters who resided at the lodge. Not all of their interactions had been good. While her partner E, her niece and nephew, and Dani might hold X in high regard, there were several others who held a heavy grudge. Just because Bennett's and Mercury's mates may not despise X, the shifters each had several scars from fighting with her.

Then there was Jace and Cassie Stockwell. X had befriended Cassie so she could capture the couple and hand them over to Madame G. The only way she helped the pair was to clue Cassie in that in order to break Madame G's hold over their mating, Cassie would need to stab Jace in the heart with their mating dagger. He resented X for that.

Rhys probably carried the worst of the scars from her. She didn't use her silver-lined blades when she could get away with it. Against the Guardians, she and E had to fight like Agents. The other Guardians might not be so forgiving, but here was proud and honorable Rhys Fitzsimmons, after all she put him through.

She owed a lot to Rhys. According to him, she owed him nothing; she was his mate, he would do whatever he needed to for her. To say he was a good male would be an understatement. He wouldn't force their mating, would wait however long she needed him to, and he wouldn't expect her to put out until she was ready.

Honestly, even after the way she had lived her life for the past twelve years, what she'd done with her body, she wasn't ready to be intimate with him, no matter how the mouthwatering male made her burn.

What the hell was her problem?

Her problem was that she survived. She had thrown away everything but her family to get to Madame G. There was supposed to be no happily ever after for her.

Yet, here he was, ready to let her into his world. In the kitchen, making her coffee that he didn't drink. He must've smelled it on her during their encounters. Oh wait…There was that one time she threw a cup in his face when the Guardians had her cornered in West Creek and she couldn't risk shooting at him in public.

"E brought your stuff from the compound. I'll make some lunch while you shower." He banged around the kitchen.

X stood up and stretched. "You saying I stink?" Silence. She grinned. "Kidding. I smell atrocious."

"You smell just fine, Alex" he rumbled from the kitchen. "It's Madame G's remnants plastered all over you that are starting to get ripe. Just drop your clothes on the sheet you slept on and I'll take them out to burn."

"Does Biggie call himself anything else now?" she called to Rhys while she stripped down.

"Nope. We tried Julio, but everyone got confused about who we were talking about, him or his son. Sometimes we say Esposito but mostly he's stuck with E."

Esposito. He'd always be Biggie to her and if he didn't like it… She suppressed a snicker. If he didn't like it, he'd know he was screwed.

"How about you?" Rhys asked, his voice barely carrying through the cabin.

She shrugged even though he couldn't see her. "As long as there's no 'Agent' in front of it." She left it at that because truth was, she didn't know.

In case he inquired further, she headed to the bathroom. The question bugged her and she chose avoidance for now.

Holy hot mess, Batman! X examined herself in the mirror. She was nearly healed, but she was covered in dirt, soot, and dried blood. Her hair was tangled in a mass of debris and sticky matter that had long dried. Underneath it all, the scars faded before her eyes, leaving only the ones previously earned from silver-laced weapons.

She jumped into the shower and mused at Rhys' sparse supplies. Soap. Razor. While he had thought of a lot of stuff for her, like her clothing and the coffee, he was still a dude and clueless as to what a girl needed in the bathroom.

"Hey! Can you bring me my bag?" she shouted as she wet down her hair.

The door opened and he tossed in a bag. If things were different and they were a real couple, she would've flashed him or stuck her leg out and invited him in. Or just walked out buck-ass naked and gotten busy with him.

They were supposed to be mates. All they needed was a ceremony to eternally bond them together. They could be a real couple at any time now, but the idea unsettled her. The thought of having sex with him, even as warmth seeped into her center, making her insides smolder for the intense male in the other room, it was…too much. She just couldn't go there. Not yet.

Wonder what Cassie would say? The human mate of the Guardian, Jace, was a shrink, but fuck if X was going to go to her and lay out her insecurities. She'd figure it out, like everything else in her life.

Murky, dirty water gradually changed to clear as she scrubbed, scraped, and lathered herself back to humanity. Or hybridity.

After drying off, she found scissors and clippers in her bag, and tackled her hair next. Instead of shaving her sides down, she tapered and blended her top into them, leaving the front half longer. They'd do a sassy sweep forward over her forehead, and when she was so inclined, she could still give herself a funky 'do.

Digging around the bag, she found her favorite pair of low-rider jeans and a pink T-shirt that read *Howl University*.

Time to face the world.

***

Rhys made sure he was gone when X stepped out of the bathroom. He left her food on the table and hoped she would stay there to eat and wouldn't roam around without him. But, she'd do whatever the hell she pleased.

He threw the bedding and clothing into the fire pit that was already working overtime with all the gear the Guardians were going through and burning from their search of Sigma's compound. Rhys headed back into his cabin.

Thank the Sweet Mother. She was sitting with her bare feet up on the kitchen table, the plate next to them already empty. One of his books was in her hands and she was fully engrossed. She looked extremely hot, even in just a simple shirt and jeans, and he liked her new cut. Full of attitude, like her.

Closing the book and tossing it on the table, she raised her brilliant eyes to him. "You want me to do the VIP visits here or out there?"

"Who do you want to talk to first?"

Her expression said no one. "Biggie, I guess."

She and E had been closer than two people should be without being mates. Hell, even closer than some mated couples he knew. Rhys jutted his chin toward the cabin they renovated for E and his family. "He's about two hundred yards behind us. Want me to go with?"

She wrinkled her nose. "Nah." Still, she exuded great reluctance.

X had written off having any life left after Madame G was destroyed. Planning a life afterward was a luxury she hadn't been able to afford. He couldn't imagine the mental mind fuck she was in now.

"Holler if you need anything."

She shot him a thumbs-up and swung her feet down. Then he watched her hips sway as she sauntered out the door wearing no shoes or socks.

Boss. Council's calling. Bennett's voice rolled through his head.

Shit.

He had sent a bare bones report that they terminated the Freemont chapter of the Sigma Network. Didn't even mention having vampires' help because he wanted to stall for time. If they found out E was part of his pack, they might demand the former Agent for punishment. But Rhys' worst fear? If they found out X was here with him. He had no idea what they'd do with her. Likely use the excuse that she was an Agent to execute her and solve their problem of what to do with her.

X wasn't the only issue. The final battle with Madame G revealed her to be a hybrid in front of many witnesses. The vampires would have just as vested of an interest in her as the shifters. It wouldn't be long before someone came to the conclusion she might have family. Then, not only would Sarah and Ronnie be in danger, but their hybrid father, X's brother John King, would be, too.

Be right there, he replied back to his second in command.

Chapter Five

X shifted uncomfortably in the little kitchen of E's cabin. She, Ana, and her former partner sat awkwardly at the table. After all the, "Hey, howya doing?" and "Can't believe we survived" shit, there wasn't a whole lot to say. It was weird. She and E had been to hell and back together, and now they could barely small talk.

Ana thanked her for being E's lifeline. X waved her off. She liked E's mate and the love shining between the two of them warmed her heart and made her want to vomit at the same time. Apparently, her lovey-dovey tolerance wasn't that high after her years with Sigma.

When Julio ran in, X tried not to yell, "Thank the Sweet Mother!" for his distraction.

"Hey X." he said, his brown eyes shining.

"'Sup dude?" X checked out how much he'd grown since she'd seen him last.

Madame G captured the kid, and she had him altered, just like his daddy. The madam was hoping he'd turn out just like E. *And he did*, X thought smugly. Goodness radiated off the kid. Though he was lanky and stronger than he knew what to do with, it was obvious his sharp mind, and good upbringing, would become a complete package of badass when he was older.

"Did you see my Lego masterpiece?" Julio darted off, and X waited to see his creation.

"Holy shit!" She had cussed without thinking when he came back, carting a large platform that housed an intricate plastic building block replica of Sigma's compound. He even built little Agents. The little bodies appeared to be defending the compound, and losing, against tiny wolves. "This is amazing, Julio."

The boy beamed under her praise.

For once, her mind wasn't on her past or present, wasn't trying to ignore her future, but marveled over Julio's handiwork. All those little figures…she could teach him maneuvers, strategy…

Ana coughed behind her hand, trying not to laugh at X's stunned reaction.

"He's got quite the imagination." Pride filled E's voice. "He's got his mother's mind. I'm trying to get him to try soccer."

"Maybe later, Dad," Julio said distractedly, rearranging the little figures.

X smirked at E, who shook his head. The guy was still getting used to being able to be an active father in Julio's life. But she got the feeling that even if he'd been able to help raise Julio from the very beginning, the two were so different, he still wouldn't know what to do with the boy.

"I gotta jet. Catch you b—" X stopped herself before saying bitches. She'd already sworn once in front of the kid. "Catch you later."

Ana's eyes twinkled as she waved at X. E walked her to the door.

"What now?" he asked.

"Dunno. You?"

He lifted one shoulder and scanned the woods. "Laying low until either council finds out about me."

"I doubt you have to worry about the vampires. They had their own people undercover, so it won't be hard for them to believe you're not a homicidal tool."

E nodded in agreement. "Demetrius said he'd take care of it. I think with the civil war rising among vampires, they're content leaving me to be the shifters' problem."

X stayed grimly silent for a few heartbeats. "I don't anticipate they'll leave me be—either council. I have an ally in Demetrius, but if he's not the victor…" X sighed. "My parents were in hiding for a reason. They didn't trust either council and neither do I. They'll find out about me soon. Then they'll go looking for John and his kids."

"Whatever happens, I'm with you, X." E's determined gaze met hers.

"No, Biggie. Whatever happens, you finally get to be with Ana and Julio." E was about to argue, but she gave him a talk-to-the-hand. "They come first. I'm not going to worry about the shitstorm coming my way until I can smell it. By the way, when I get a car, you get to clean it. I totally won the bet about Madame G's shoes."

E rolled his eyes. "Prove it."

"Don't tell me you didn't look when I took her down. I know you were in the trees with the rest."

He narrowed his eyes, trying to hide a smile. "Maybe."

She gave him a friendly punch in the shoulder before she left and headed out into the woods. Her mind wandered. She had felt edgy when she woke up. After seeing E, the feeling intensified. It was great viewing him in his new little home with his beautiful family. It was everything they had fought for.

So why did she feel so…restless?

Squinting up through the leaves, she headed toward a familiar tract of land that bordered the Guardians' property. The sun was bright and the air crisp enough that if she stopped, she'd get cold. Her bare feet enjoyed maneuvering through the brittle undergrowth, while her eyes savored the shade of the multicolored autumn leaves.

It was fucking gorgeous. Her heart twisted as an unbidden memory rose. Her father, laughing next to her one late summer day, as they wandered in the trees around the house she'd grown up in. They each had a camera and took pictures of the turning leaves for her vampire mother, since she couldn't be out in daylight. It hadn't been significant to her then, just something sweet her father had done for her mother. Now, she marveled at how accepting her dad had been of her mom's nature. Two beings, from two separate worlds, trying to raise a happy, healthy family.

And they had succeeded, X thought mournfully. Her brother John had found his mate in a human woman who was willing to live in secrecy with him and raise their kids. Some of X's fondest moments were of running around, playing games with little Sarah and Ron.

Then one dark day, it was all taken away from them.

X frowned, barely noticing where her feet stepped, just following her senses, lost in thought.

She and her parents had been heading back to their house in the country. They had driven far out on nearly forgotten roads to shift and run their wolves without being seen or sensed by others. It was after dark, so her vampire mother could run with them.

The ambush had been sudden and devastating.

Agents rammed their car. Taking advantage of their disorientation, they pumped silver bullets into both of her parents before beheading them. She tried getting away, but an eighteen-year-old stood little chance against trained fighters.

Her mom had just fed from her father after their run and smelled like a shifter. Madame G never suspected X was the hybrid she'd been searching for, just a little shifter prize for her to torment.

Agents hid the murder by burning the bodies in the car, then pushing it deep into the trees. It had all happened in such a remote place, X wondered if they were ever found. Not that whoever found the scene of the crime could make out any details. The Agents had made sure of it.

It had been pure stubbornness that she didn't cave to Madame G's every demand those first two years she was captive. Stubbornness and cleverness. She had remained astute enough to hypnotize the males Madame G sent her way and take their blood. Yes, she could've mesmerized them into leaving her alone, but then she would've been caught. So she sacrificed her body for her mind.

Why the fuck was she treading down memory lane? Those memories hadn't plagued her for over a decade.

X strode through woods, making little noise. It was not that she was trying to act like a stalking predator, it was just automatic at this point. She came upon a clearing in the trees and sensed her target working in the gardens.

A straw hat hovered a few feet off the ground as the slight body underneath was picked the last of the harvest.

Sarah Young tensed when she sensed another presence, but the young hybrid straightened with a big smile on her face.

She squealed and ran toward X. "Auntie Allie!"

X couldn't help but grin. Sarah used to do the same thing when she five. Now twenty years later, it was like nothing had changed.

Her niece flung herself into X's arms. Laughing sobs were muffled by X's shirt.

"I'm sorry." Sarah drew back, wiping at her eyes. "I just didn't think you'd want to see me."

X's brow drew down in confusion. "Why the hell not?"

Sarah blinked. "It's just that, you know, we wrote you off as dead."

Pinning the girl with a stern look, she asked, "Do you hold it against me that they went after you, thinking you were the hybrid they were hunting while I was under their nose the whole time?"

"Of course not," Sarah said horrified.

Her niece sniffled and stood awkwardly, and yeah, this totally was the theme to X's day. Awkward.

"You've really grown, kid."

Sarah grinned. "Yeah."

X scanned the little farm that Sarah and her brother cared for. "So…Bennett Young, huh?"

A pretty blush stained Sarah's obviously happy face. "Yeah."

"Isn't he kind of a dick?"

Sarah's grin widened. "Yeah." She sounded completely, hopelessly in love.

Squinting even more, now that she was clear of the trees, X wished she thought to bring a pair of sunglasses for her sensitive hybrid eyes. She didn't turn to ash like full-blooded vampires, but she would require a little extra blood from the sun damage. Rhys would willingly give it; it would be an erotic experience. And X didn't really want to revisit that anytime soon.

Why not?

Good question. Erotic was an understatement. Being in that male's arms was…earth-shattering. And they'd both been fully clothed. The thought of doing it again should make her feel heady, powerful, but it made her feel panicked.

X eyed her niece. "How do you stand it, working out in the sun all day?"

They were polar opposites. Sarah was much shorter, with sun-bleached honey-brown hair. X could see a lot of her brother in Sarah's features.

"Well," Sarah gestured up to her wide-brimmed straw hat, "this helps. I used to keep a couple of cows around to feed from, but now that I have Bennett…" Another smile plastered her face. "We keep Bessie and Tulip around for Ronnie. He bitches about it, but I know he'd rather bite through leather than have to risk finding a human vein."

"How is Ron?" X had kept tabs on him after he had come to Freemont. Madame G hunted him, trying to get to Sarah, but he was a crafty bastard and got himself committed to a psyche ward to keep out of her clutches. After Bennett found Sarah, they busted Ron out of the mental hospital, and X had breathed a sigh of relief.

"He's in the house if you want to see him." Sarah pointed to the newly-built house on the property. The original structure had burned to the ground when Sigma had tried to capture Sarah. "He's pickling peppers and canning salsa to sell at the market."

As X searched for her nephew, she decided she might go for a run afterward. She wanted to say hey to Ron, but she also wanted to get the hell out of there and go somewhere else. Somewhere with no people.

She entered the kitchen in time to hear a male voice say, "Pop my little pretties. Pop!"

Ron stood at the counter with his arms raised over some mason jars filled with salsa. They had just been taken out of their canning bath. He spun around when he heard the door shut. A giant German shepherd charged her, barking ferociously.

"Apollo, stop." The mighty dog skidded to a halt at Ron's command, studying X warily.

She eyed him back before turning her attention to her nephew. He was a man, but he had such boyish features, it was easy to remember the fun little boy he used to be.

"Aunt Allie…Agent…uh, X?" He finally gave up.

"Whatevs. Except for the Agent bit. We can leave that off."

He nodded and they stood—wait for it— awkwardly, only the pops of the jars sealing themselves made any sound.

X finally filled in the silence. "Just came to say he-eeey."

"Hey," Ron said back, shoving his hands in his pockets. "Do Mom and Dad know you're alive yet?"

Shit. Did they? "I haven't talked to them. Maybe it'd be better coming from you or Sarah." And fuck. If the meet and greets today were nearly unbearable to get through, then what would reuniting with her brother and his wife be like?

And these were the people who used to love her. Maybe they still did, but in all fairness, they didn't really know her any more. What would coming across the Guardians be like? Or worse, the son of the seer who was killed?

Time to go.

"Nice to see you again, Ron."

He bobbed his shaggy yellow-blond mop of hair. "You too, X."

She almost sighed. Not even two minutes together and he used her letter, too. He associated that with her, more than the aunt who had twirled him around when he was a toddler.

Maybe a run in the woods would clear her head.

***

"He's served us well. He's proven his allegiance." Rhys addressed the council on the computer monitor. For being such a crusty, old-fashioned lot, they certainly didn't mind using technology to rag on his ass.

"And who does Agent E hold allegiance to?" Councilman Seether asked silkily.

All five council members were glaring through the monitor at Rhys.

"Me. And he's no longer an Agent."

Murmurs erupted and a few of the members sat back.

Councilmen Wallace, the father of the twins in Rhys' pack, spoke next. "I don't know that it's a good idea to have one such as this *former* Agent at your disposal. He's committed atrocities against our people."

Rhys expected that argument. "The alleged crimes committed against our kind were reported to be in regards to rogue or feral shifters, or those working as spies for the Sigma Network. There have been no reports of E killing an innocent shifter." Hurting maybe, but X and her partner had ridden a fine line.

"That may be so," Councilman Seether replied, "but only Guardians are allowed to deal with those transgressions. He is neither shifter, nor Guardian. In fact, he is an abomination created by a mad, deranged vampire."

The councilman's tone suggested that he, and the rest of the council, thought that an abomination should be eradicated.

"Julio Esposito Senior is an altered human who worked diligently for over a decade to overthrow

Madame G. He and his family have become part of this pack."

Sharp inhales hissed through the monitor. Only human mates were allowed to become part of a pack. It was unheard of to adopt an entire human family into a shifter pack. What the council didn't know was that Ana and Julio were also no longer entirely human.

"Unmated humans can't belong to a pack," Councilman Seether spit out.

Was he disgusted because of the unmated part or the human part? Rhys and his pack more than suspected that the council was behind certain acts that would keep the shifter species pure and free from human interbreeding to keep shifter blood strong.

"E has been shown to carry shifter genetics. I would prefer to honor the shifters who died in Madame G's captivity by not throwing away E's life."

"Honor?" Councilman Wallace snorted. Like Seether, he was a distinguished-looking male, graying around the temples, with fierce eyes. "To honor them would be throw Agent E behind bars for the rest of his life, at the very least."

Before Rhys could reply, another member of the council spoke up. A quiet male, but very shrewd from the way he narrowed in on Rhys. "Agent E carries both shifter and vampire genes. A hybrid of sorts. That brings up an interesting rumor we heard."

Ice crystals settled into Rhys' veins. How did they find out about X so soon? Was it the vampires, or one of the shifter captives they released? He didn't think Demetrius would sink so low as to use X to get the Lycan Council off his back while he battled his own vampire leadership. But the vampire *was* a self-serving ass, so maybe…

"A pure hybrid of a vampire and shifter mating," Councilman Hargrath continued, "one who was at Madame G's disposal?"

The council sure didn't seem surprised that there was a real hybrid running around. All his long life, Rhys had been taught it was genetically impossible. Vampires and shifters hated each other. Yet the council's lack of surprise, and the way X's family had lived in secrecy, made Rhys think that there were no hybrids because they were either prevented or destroyed.

He knew it would come to this; he couldn't hide her existence forever.

"The former Agent X has displayed abilities of both vampire and shifter. She is still recovering from the final battle. Until she's healed, I won't know more." He had pre-chosen his words, extremely grateful the council couldn't smell his deceit in a video conference.

"She's extremely dangerous," Councilman Seether hissed.

"Like E, she was also working against Sigma. According to the seer before she died, X was targeted because she signaled the downfall of Madame G."

"You will interrogate the female?" Councilman Hargrath sat forward, glaring into the monitor.

Stark relief draped over Rhys. The council didn't know, yet, that X was his mate. Shit would hit the fan when the council discovered it. Then, Rhys' credibility regarding X *and* her partner would be shredded, and they would want to deal with the former Agents themselves. For now, he could act as a buffer and stall for time.

"We will find out everything when she recovers." And *they* would find out nothing. X's brother was still living in hiding with his wife. Sarah and Ronnie would be highly sought after by the council, even with hybrid blood diluted by their human mother.

"Learn her familial origins," Councilman Hargrath ordered. "Find out if she has any siblings, children. Sweet Mother only knows how that madwoman must've tried to breed her."

Rhys ground down so hard his teeth should've cracked. Madame G didn't know X carried shifter and vampire blood, but she would've watched X for any sign of pregnancy. She most definitely would've provided enough partners, consensual or not. Thankfully, young born outside of a mating bond were extremely rare and female shifters' fertile cycles were years apart. That had both saved and condemned many female shifters in the madam's clutches. Once deemed useless, they were fed to the vampires.

"I'll notify you when I have information," Rhys replied dutifully, hoping he could just delay them and sign-off.

"And about Agent E?" Councilman Seether prompted.

"E remains my responsibility."

"He should face a tribunal." The other council members nodded their agreement.

As if E would get a fair trial.

"Esteemed council," Rhys wasn't above kissing ass for the safety of his pack, "I ask that you give me time to gather the history and information on the hybrid, before we discuss what will be decided with E."

"It's too dangerous to have those two within close proximity of each other. Their reputation together was formidable."

"They worked extremely well together as a pair," Rhys agreed. "Yet in the years I've fought them, we all avoided mortally wounding one another. I believe it would be ill-advised to apprehend E and treat him like a threat while trying to gain cooperation from his partner."

Ill-advised was an understatement. X's status as his destined mate would mean nothing if E's life was threatened. She would assume all the danger to protect E's family as she methodically incapacitated the council until E was free.

A moment of tense silence passed before Councilman Seether finally acquiesced. "Very well. We expect a full report of what you have, and a proposal of how you plan to proceed, in two days' time."

Rhys' hit the exit button and breathed a sigh of relief. Two days to figure out what the hell to do.

***

X wandered through the woods. She roamed around, soaking in the quiet beauty, but didn't transition to her wolf form like she had planned. The thought of running through the woods on four legs made her almost as agitated as the first round of visits had done.

Yes, she had run as a wolf since she was captured. But it was only out of necessity and always where Madame G couldn't see. The more it slipped the mad bitch's mind that X could shift, the better. After those first couple of years when the madam forced transitions for her study, X always felt unease at the thought of shifting. Anticipation of what bad things would follow a shift diminished, but never left her.

So here she was, walking barefoot through the trees, letting her mind wander. She thought about everything and nothing at all.

A delightful scent tickled her nose.

He was close.

She waited for him to get closer before stopping and facing his direction. An extremely large, red-tinted wolf stood in the trees, as if awaiting her permission to come closer.

Rhys was magnificent, even covered in fur. She hoped he stayed in wolf form almost as much as she hoped he'd shift so she could get a full view of his powerful body.

He stared at her as if to ask if she was all right; he didn't have to mind-speak.

"I'm fine. Wanna walk back with me?"

Rhys blinked his answer and waited for her to turn and head back. He padded through the trees next to her.

Did you meet with anyone?

"Yeah." She didn't bother with mentally speaking to him. She could sense that it was only the two of them and they were miles from his cabin.

He didn't ask how it went, noticing the unease in X. She could see him out of the corner of her eye, filtering through the leaves and branches as he kept pace with her. Maybe she'd run her wolf tomorrow.

Maybe not.

She was really tired. It occurred to her that she woke up from healing, but hadn't had any real rest in weeks. Years.

"When we get back, I'm gonna bunk down for a nap." X didn't know why she announced it. Just felt like he should know.

His concern emanated off him, but she didn't explain any further. She could go find Dani, do another hey-how-are-ya, maybe chance a meeting with one of the Guardians in her new role as their leader's soon-to-be-mate. Yet, she didn't because she didn't want to.

The well of disquiet rose again. She should be jumping for joy. She was free of Sigma, free to mate the most magnificent male she'd ever met, free to do a whole lotta shit. And it all made her stomach turn. Why? She'd been in a lot of stomach-turning situations, why was the good stuff bothering her?

Like before, no answers were coming to her, so she just kept walking, aiming for Rhys' cabin and that bed.

Chapter Six

The cabin was empty when X rose the next day. Her nap turned into a solid fifteen hours of sleep. She hadn't even stirred when Rhys had climbed into bed with her. Being accustomed to his presence in her dreams kept her from jolting awake, shoving a blade deep into his belly. Which he'd probably take in stride, understanding her reaction and what had honed her reflexes.

X sighed and ran a hand through her hair. Like usual, Rhys did nothing but protect her dreams until he had to go to work in the morning. They hadn't said a word to each other since their walk in the woods.

After cleaning up and changing into a fresh pair of pants and a new shirt that read, *If you can read this, quit looking at my boobs*, X wandered into the small kitchen. She found a pot of coffee waiting for her and a few breakfast items to choose from. Rhys either ate most of his food at the lodge or in his office, because it certainly wasn't in the cabin. It appeared he did a quick stock for her and that was it.

X wrinkled her nose and poured herself some coffee. The idea of going to the lodge to eat with everyone else was akin to peeling skin off her forearms. So she grabbed pretty much everything and ate it all, slowly draining the entire pot of brew.

With caffeinated veins and a belly full of processed crap, she charged out the door, sans shoes again. Her skin brushing against leaves and branches centered her. Growing up, shifting had been severely limited. She and her brother had run barefoot to stay linked to nature.

Steeling herself, she hiked toward Dani's cabin. The question of whether anyone was home or not was answered by a crash from inside. Frowning, X trotted up the porch and listened briefly before knocking on the door.

It swung open to reveal a flustered Dani. Her eyes brightened when they landed on her guest. "X!" Another thud. Alarm crossed over Dani's face as she spun away, leaving the door open for X.

Dani rushed into a main seating area and picked up a smiley bundle of baby. She propped him on her hip and bounced side to side. Books fallen off the bookshelves were strewn across the floor.

"This is Dante," Dani said, rhythmically swaying left and right while the little boy with bronze highlights in his brown hair fisted a handful of Dani's dark locks. "He's a little...he's gifted."

X examined the books and clutter around the rest of the cabin. If by gifted, she meant Dante was already displaying telekinetic power like his daddy and loved throwing things off shelves, the evidence was easy to see.

"He's displaying his powers early, huh?"

"Yeah." Dani sounded flustered, exasperated, and extremely proud. "Mercury can help calm him, but he's still learning how to use his own abilities. Mostly we end up being damage control."

X nodded. She had heard and seen the evidence of how the Guardians' powers had been failing them. When they began finding their mates, they regained control and strength. Mercury's abilities were much more powerful than most shifters, and from the looks of the cabin, so were little Dante's.

Dani waved her to a chair. "Have a seat. I can't promise nothing will fly into you."

X's mouth quirked up. Dante must make the days exciting. He wasn't even a year old yet. Most supernaturals didn't gain use of their abilities until after puberty, when there was some hope they could control them. X wondered how full Dani's and Mercury's hands must be trying to raise a gifted baby.

"So, uh, how's it going?" Dani set the boy back down to crawl around on the floor. He instantly crawled to X.

"It's going." It was all X said, watching the baby inspect her toes and then use her pants to gain footing so he could try to stand. She smiled inwardly. Babies were so cute and innocent.

"I'm grateful for everything you taught me. I don't hold any grudges, you know, for capturing Mercury," Dani said reassuringly.

"Good to know." X's awkwardness returned. She'd rather roll around on the floor with Dante making choo-choo noises than have this discussion.

When she and E had been in charge of Dani's training in Sigma, the girl had been so full of questions, so willing to learn. It had been obvious Dani was wrong for Sigma, and X respected the hell out of her for getting away. She just didn't know what to sit and talk about.

"How's it going with you?" X asked, before the silence stretched on for too long.

A cloud crossed the young woman's face. "Good."

She was lying. "You sure?"

Dani blinked. "No. It's wonderful, it really is. It's just…" She took a deep breath. "I'm pregnant again."

It was X's turn to blink. "Wow. Congrats?"

Drawing in a shaky breath, Dani put a hand lovingly over her abdomen. "Yeah, it is great. It's just scary. Terrifying. Shifters don't usually have young this close together, and Dante has such strong abilities, and I feel so damn unqualified to raise powerful babies. And…" Dani sucked in a ragged breath. "We haven't told anyone else, but…it's twins."

Whoa. "So you're a little stressed?"

"That's an understatement," Dani said, nodding.

Heavy boots climbed the steps outside. Dani's face brightened as X stiffened. The front door opened to reveal a hulk of a male with dark hair that gleamed silver. The same silver glittered through the male's eyes as he took in X sitting in his living quarters, hanging out with his mate and kid.

"'Sup, Merc?" Drool pooled onto X's foot as Dante laughed and bounced at the sight of his father.

Mercury's gaze warmed when they landed upon his son, then trailed down to the drool and back up to X. It was like he was waiting to see her reaction at getting baby body fluids on her.

Please, baby drool was the tamest body fluid she'd encountered.

Standing up, she bent down, winking at Dante when his bronze gleaming eyes caught hers. She gently dislodged him from her leg.

Mercury was still tense, Dani's mouth tightened in irritation at her mate, but she knew the history, and only waited for the confrontation to play out.

Dante babbled happily where X had set him down.

"You have a beautiful family, Mercury." She made her way to the door.

"I know." He eyed her warily and stepped aside to let her pass.

"Catch you later, Dani." Stepping across the threshold, X turned and caught the door before it closed all the way. The muscles in Mercury's chest flexed. Irritation at his reaction glinted in Dani's eyes. "For what it's worth, Dani, my mom talked about how nursery rhymes would soothe little vampires when their urges would get to be too much for them. She said singing helped me and my brother calm down when our eyes would get the vampire-red glow." X left without waiting for a response.

She really wished she could get down on the floor and hang with the baby. Just like Julio and his Legos were the best part of the previous day, she suspected seeing a cute, chubby baby would be the only highlight of today.

Stepping off the porch, X decided to walk back to Rhys' cabin and…totally not hide. Read, maybe. Would it kill Rhys to get a TV or something? Hell, even a radio. The silence in the cabin was going to drive her batshit, otherwise. She needed to watch *Jeopardy* or something to keep her mind occupied.

She was halfway back when movement caught her eye. In an instant, a throwing knife was in one hand and ready to go. A young male stepped from behind a tree. His pale hair and pale-blue eyes was so much like his seer mother. X lowered her hand.

They stood staring at each other for a long time. She hadn't encountered him his entire time at Sigma. Madame G had kept him secret and highly protected. And in all truth, X and E ensured they got assignments that took them away from the compound often, for as long as possible.

A trace of ever-present guilt laced through her mind. If she and E had been around more, maybe they would've heard that a young shifter had been studied, tortured. A little interference, a small accident and oops he escaped…They could've done something to help the kid get away.

His hands started moving, and X tensed, her hand closing tighter on her knife. She held back a scowl at her reaction and sheathed her knife. He was still a damn kid, barely eighteen. Even if he did attack her, she wasn't going to hurt him.

He was communicating to her in sign language. She shook her head. "Sorry. I don't understand what you're saying."

He frowned and slumped his shoulders, his pale hair falling into his face. He was tall like most shifters, and carried a good amount of muscle, but it was clear he still had more filling out to do.

She'd been so preoccupied with his appearance, and who his mother was, that the details of his scent finally registered.

A Guardian. No wonder he'd been kept here after Mercury rescued him.

She wanted to laugh. That would really piss off the Lycan Council. Parrish's pale coloring indicated he was a seer. A seer who was a Guardian. A seer who the council couldn't completely control.

Did she suffer?

X was startled by the voice filtering through her mind. "What do you mean?"

She always tried to console me, told me lies to make things seem better than they were. Was she suffering the whole time? The kid's head hung even more, and he rubbed at his temples, like the effort was giving him a headache.

Oh hell. X would take two more months of maladroit visiting over this experience. "Uhhh, I don't know." He glanced up at her perplexed; she shrugged. "None of us knew about her until a few weeks ago. But when I saw her, she seemed well-cared for."

His hands dropped to wipe at his eyes, and he sniffled.

She didn't know much of his history, just what Rhys had passed on. The kid had spent most of his life at Sigma, and it had only been the last few years that were miserable for him.

"I can tell you that we tried to save her." At her words, he yanked his head up, his pale-blue eyes anguished. "She was ready to go. She knew it was her time, and that you were where you needed to be."

He considered her for a minute before nodding and dropping his gaze. Her heart wasn't so jaded that it didn't go out to the kid. He was a seer. He must've known it wouldn't end well for his mother.

She felt a tickle at her mind like he was going to telepathically say something else, when they were interrupted.

"Parrish, you doing okay?" Bennett Young strode smoothly out of the shadows, eying X like a coiled cobra.

As if she'd hurt a kid.

Parrish ducked his head, his hands flying. X would bite her tongue until she drew blood before she asked Bennett what Parrish was saying.

"He's says he's sorry." Bennett snapped his gaze back to X. "Why does he look like he's in pain?"

X snorted. "Cuz you're here," she shot back at him.

Parrish was waving his hands, brushing off Bennett's concerns.

"Why do you have a headache?" Bennett asked him. To X he asked, "Were you trying to hypnotize him?"

Bennett thought she mind-blasted the kid? "Fuck you." X shot back at him without thinking. Well, this day was going down the shitter.

"It's not *me* you're fucking with," Bennett hissed at her.

She cocked her head at him. What the hell did he mean?

"Parrish." Bennett didn't take his eyes off her. "Head back to the lodge."

The kid was about to argue. Instead, he shot X an apologetic look and followed Bennett's orders.

Crossing her arms over her chest, she waited for Bennett to elaborate.

"Look," he ran a hand through his hair, "I get you're Sarah's aunt. And you're supposed to be the commander's mate. But," he shook his head, "he didn't think we saw, you know, how crazy you made him. I helped patch him up after his fights with you. Hell, we all carry scars from you."

"Are you dead?"

Bennett scowled at her.

"Exactly," she kept going before he responded. "Rhys understands. I did what I had to do."

"And what if you have to do something in the future and Sarah gets hurt?"

X clenched her jaw, her anger flaring. Mostly because he hit a nerve. "I protected her and Ron the best I could."

"You protected yourself even more." Bennett's navy-blue eyes matched her ire. "I respect Commander Fitzsimmons. He wants you as a mate. Whatever. But I don't want to find myself patching up Sarah's wounds because of you."

"And what does Sarah have to say?"

Bennett's eyes flicked away briefly, the only indication that his mate had no idea he was confronting X. "I already had to moderate a fight between her and Ronnie after you left yesterday."

X recoiled in shock. They were fighting? Over her?

Bennett nodded. "Seems you stopped by. She thought Ronnie said something to piss you off since you left so abruptly. Then they were arguing about what to tell their father about the sister he thinks is dead."

It hit X that she was leaving a heavy burden on her family's shoulders. Honestly, she wasn't much older than each of them, but it felt like decades.

"I'll call John tonight," she said quietly.

Bennett didn't reply right away. If he was surprised by her offer, he didn't show it. Finally, he nodded. "Don't screw over the commander. If he goes down, I'll have to lead this team, and then I'll be really pissed at you."

Bennett started walking away when X called after him. "Hey Benji." She'd heard Mercury refer to him as that once, so X did, too. Mostly because it irritated him. "You realize I'm your aunt now, right?"

She sensed his irritation spike and it made her laugh. He didn't stop to acknowledge the point she made. *Suck on that, Benji.*

***

"I need your phone."

Rhys had just stepped into his cabin. X lowered the book she was reading to look up at him through her hair. He liked the new cut, but it covered more of her face than usual.

"Okay." He tossed it to her.

"And there's a number I need."

When she told him, he shouldn't have been as surprised as he felt. He had the number ready, just in case. Her brother's number changed frequently, and he always knew the latest digits in case Sarah or Ronnie needed to get hold of their parents.

Then she went out to the back deck for some privacy.

Rhys set the bag he brought home on the table. He had a strong hunch that X wouldn't want to eat at the lodge with the rest of his pack, so he grabbed some burgers and fixings, and packed them to go.

He waited to eat until X came back twenty minutes later. Her face was ashen, shoulders not as square. No tears stained her cheeks, but he wished they did. Then it would mean that she let some emotion through.

"Have a seat." He warmed up some food and set it in front of her.

"Thanks," she mumbled, and went about eating like a robot zombie.

Rhys didn't even bother with conversation, just cleaned up the meal when they were done.

"Will you…" Her gaze landed on the floor, her brow creased deep. "Can you…lie with me? Like you usually do?"

She wasn't asking for sex. She wasn't asking for anything more than spooning on the bed.

He took off his gear, kicked off his boots, and followed her lithe form into the bedroom. Crawling into the bed, he wrapped his arms around her, angling his hips back so she wouldn't feel the ever-present erection he had around her. The last thing he wanted was for her to feel pressured into anything intimate she wasn't ready for.

But that day, over a month ago in the woods, before she helped E escape Sigma, that day would get him through many nights. It already had. The feel of her lips wrapped around him, cupping his—

Yeah, so not the time.

Occasionally, he would feel her blink where her head lay on his arm. Eventually, she drifted off to sleep, and he followed her in to protect her dreams, anticipating a more nightmare-filled sleep than usual.

***

"It's been two days, Commander. What do you have?" Councilman Seether rasped into the monitor.

Rhys smoothly rattled off his reply while Bennett observed. He figured he'd better have another Guardian clued in to what was going on with the council. Later, he would bounce ideas off Master Bellamy, since he was commander before Rhys, and might have more insight into how to handle the crusty bastards.

Telling them nothing more than how X was captured, he described the scene. He'd seen it enough in her dreams. He detailed what he knew of her time with Sigma and how she partnered with E, in hopes that they could work together to defeat Madame G.

"That's what I have for now," Rhys concluded. "I'll work on getting more details."

"Don't you have a family name?" Councilmen Hargrath asked, with too much interest for Rhys' liking.

Rhys was even more grateful Bennett was with him. The other Guardian needed to know what his own mate might face—the too avid interest from the council.

"It's coming. She's working on remembering the details of her history."

Several members of the council shifted in their chairs. A few exchanged unreadable looks.

"And Agent E. Has he shown any penchant for malice?" Councilman Seether asked.

"None. I fully believe he is in his right mind."

Councilman Hargrath leaned into the camera. "Why is he of sound mind and Agent X is not?"

"E was a grown man when he was abducted and converted into an Agent. X was still a teenager, and she was put through rigorous...efforts...to make her agree to become an Agent."

Harrumphs and throat clearing could be heard as they digested that. It was a good sign, a sign that they were seeing E and X in a different light, and not just as Agents.

"How long do you anticipate this," Councilman Seether waved his hand, "amnesia?" His tone was almost a sneer. Rhys wished he could reach through the camera and wring his wiry little neck.

"Unknown. Give me another week to work with her and report back."

More looks were exchanged before the council grudgingly acquiesced.

Clicking off and shutting down the computer for good measure, Rhys turned to Bennett.

"What are we going to do?" Bennett asked.

Rhys knew the male's fear was for Sarah, and with good reason. Keeping X a secret was risky. If they discovered her and started digging into her past, they'd figure out Sarah used to go by Spencer and is X's niece.

"For now, keep stalling."

"Does X know they know about her?"

Rhys sighed and scrubbed his face. He slept like shit, constantly being roused by X's nightmares. He left his lovely mate sleeping in their bed this morning so he could come answer to the council.

"No. It's not really on her mind right now, with everything else."

Bennett remained ominously silent.

"What?" Rhys demanded irritably.

The blond male threw his hands up in a helpless gesture. "What is right. We need to tell the council something, like X's entire family is dead and she wants to be your little mate and live happily ever after. Make up some bullshit last name, forge some records, whatever. Or, we need to own that we're hiding hybrids—a whole family of hybrids—and deal with the fallout. This isn't just about X."

"You think I don't know that?" Tension coiled tightly in his gut, and Bennett was standing on the release lever.

Both males felt strongly that they couldn't trust the council to have X and her family's best interests in mind. Not with a strong suspicion that the shifters on the Lycan Council had interfered with several packs, possibly killing members in the name of protecting bloodlines.

"You know it, but you're letting X cloud your duties as pack leader."

Before a coherent thought formed in Rhys' mind, he had Bennett hauled up out of his chair and shoved up against the wall. The male's eyes blazed blue fire, while Rhys' own burned with his anger and frustration.

"Think about what she's been through. Think!" Rhys shoved at Bennett, again wanting to shake the male. To the blonde's credit, he didn't fight back, sensing he'd pushed his commander too far. "When your first mate turned on you and you were tortured for her betrayal…remember? That was nothing compared to what Alexandria King was put through. Hell, it was nothing compared to what she went through as an Agent. So, yeah, if she needs some extra time to get her shit together and figure out what the hell she's gonna do in this world, then I'm going to make sure she gets all the time she needs."

Rhys abruptly let go and stepped back, his body coiled, ready, in case Bennett reacted.

Bennett warily regarded Rhys as he straightened his clothes. "If that's what she needs, so be it. But after dealing with X and E for the last however-many years, I'm not ready to assume now that Madame G's gone, they'll be picture perfect citizens. I can't trust that they're not sitting back, waiting to see which way the wind blows, and forming a plan in their minds where the end justifies the means."

Anger spiked in Rhys again, but he forced himself to remain still. Bennett was allowed his opinion, and dammit, he was watching out for the pack. Up until a few weeks ago, X and her partner had been the bad guys.

He glared at Bennett. "We have a week. You can at least give her that."

Chapter Seven

S ilence.
　　That's what X had gotten on the other end of the phone when she had called her brother. Her end of the conversation was basically, "Hey bro, guess what? I'm really alive. After two years of torture, I became one of the best Agents ever so I could finally kill Madame G. Wow, the kids have really grown, right?"

John hadn't stuttered, sputtered, or bombarded her with questions. There was silence, followed by an even, "Whose body was in the car with Mom and Dad?"

"Probably a recruit who wasn't performing. Sigma loved the old switcheroo trick."

It's how Madame G faked E's death. It obviously worked. Since her family couldn't call the cops and forensics wasn't an option, she could see how three bodies burned beyond recognition would be pretty convincing.

"Anyhoo, I'm laying low. Why don't you give Sarah or Ron a call?"

"Alexandria—"

X had hung up before listening to anything more and sat gazing out at the night after that. She hadn't known what John was going to say, but honestly, she couldn't take suspicion from him. Not after what she'd been through.

Then she went inside and, in a moment of weakness, asked Rhys to damn near rock her to sleep. Ugh. Three days out of Sigma and she was already a gigantic pussy.

Her mate had kept her nightmares at bay and she'd gotten a ton of sleep. But now she was restless, edgy. Again.

A whole day of wandering the cabin did not make for a happy X. She was tired of reading and it felt like the walls were closing in on her. But it was better than heading out the door and running into anyone. She just didn't want to deal with that shit right now.

Rhys stormed into the cabin, his face clouded, looking like he'd had a shitty day at work. The door slammed behind him. They both stared at each other, their primal need for each other flared strong. She found an outlet for her restless energy, and her only source of comfort was in his arms.

Without saying a word, she floated over to him. He watched her advance, letting her set the pace.

When she reached him, she snaked her arms around his neck. His smoldering hazel eyes lit with more green than brown, gaining intensity as the scent of desire increased.

She let her fangs drop and nipped at his lip, liking his groan as she lapped at the drop of blood that the sharp point drew.

He tried to hold back, but she felt his resistance crumble as he bent his head down and captured her mouth, pulling her tightly against him. The steel length of him pressed into her belly and she enjoyed the delicious feeling of his solid body and warm, hot mouth.

It was her first real kiss.

She'd used her mouth for a lot of things over the years, but kissing passionately had never been one of them. Before life with Sigma, her teenage years included only a few chaste pecks with the gangly boy who took her to homecoming.

This was hot, it was intoxicating, and the intimacy was almost too much to bear.

As if sensing she was about to freeze up, he drew his mouth down her neck, laying sweltering kisses on her sensitized skin. He lifted her shirt to get his hands onto her bare skin while she worked his shirt up above his shoulders. He broke away from her only to shrug out of his shirt and toss it to the side.

She loved the way his muscles bulged and flexed as he leaned down to cup her bottom and lift her. X wrapped her jean-clad legs around him, wondering how decadent it would feel to have no clothing separating them. Burying her face into his neck, she clung to him, deftly licking the skin she planned to bite.

"Fuck, yes," he rasped.

Turning her until her back hit the wall, he pressed into her and she ground into him. She struck, her fangs sinking in to find his sweet vein. He hissed, but it was far from agony. His rigid length pulsed against her abdomen.

She only took a few mouthfuls before she was overwhelmed, the power more than she could handle. The scent of his arousal, the heat blazing through her body, the pulse between her legs—she needed more.

Sensually licking over the puncture wounds, she gave them a little kiss. He groaned and undulated his hips into her, seeking some release to the pressure building inside him.

X lifted her head, looking up at him through her lashes. His face was tight with desire, his breathing heavy. Beneath her touch, muscles quivered from holding himself back.

"I want more," she whispered.

His eyes flared, but instead of rushing to strip them both down, he proceeded with care, giving her plenty of time to call a time-out.

Lifting her shirt higher, he pulled it off and dropped it beside them; his stare ate up the view. She wore a standard black bra, nothing fancy, but the way his gaze burned made it seem like it was the most expensive scrap of lace.

With deliberate slowness, he slid his hand behind her. She arched her back for him, pressing her breasts into his chest. He unhooked her bra and dropped it to the floor, next to the shirt. She pressed against the wall and he leaned back, seeking an unburdened view of her assets.

"They're perfect." His hands cupped each breast, his thumbs brushing her nipples. A shiver traveled down her spine.

"They're big." She arched into him, his hands were so warm and doing the most wonderful things.

"I know. Perfect."

Rhys bent his head, licking his way down to one nipple, then pulling it into his mouth. X ran her fingers through his short, russet hair, a moan escaping her when his teeth gently tugged at her tender flesh.

He turned his attention to the other breast and she used the opportunity to stroke his muscles. He was a male in his prime, a warrior, and he had the scars to prove it. His skin was hot and solid, like steel lined his bones. How long had she admired his broad, muscular shoulders? Now she could touch them to her heart's desire.

Her body needed even more, his blood ignited every nerve ending in it. Unwrapping her legs from his waist, she placed her feet on the floor and gently pushed at him until he lifted his face to her. His eyes were hooded, dangerous in their smoldering intensity.

X ran her hands down his chest, enjoying every inch of rippled flesh along the way, until her hands ran over a pale rigid scar that crossed his right side.

He froze. Her fingers played over the ridge. It was a knife wound, one that ran deep, with scarring that could only be caused by silver.

"I didn't mean to cut so deeply," she admitted.

It had been their first meeting, their first fight. She and E were more than a little concerned facing Guardians, so when the ripple of awareness that the mighty male she faced-off with was her destined mate…well, her reflexes took over and she shanked him. With a silver-lined blade, no less. She was only barely able to pull back so she didn't completely puncture his liver, causing him to bleed out before healing could begin.

"I wear my scars from you with pride."

His said it so openly, so completely honest. She knew exactly what he meant. Her scars were minimal, any silver-made wounds not scarring as badly thanks to her vampire half, but she earned every one. Each one she earned from a Guardian, especially Rhys, was one that hadn't killed her.

Her fingers played over the twisted flesh.

"Does it cause you pain?" she asked.

There was a hitch in his breathing, and she knew the answer.

Again, he was honest. "Sometimes it makes itself known."

"I'll have to make up for that."

Leaning down, she ran her tongue down the length of the pale scar. He drew in a sharp breath and dug his hands into her hair.

Not stopping at the end of the long scar, she kneeled as she ran her tongue down to the waistband of his black cargo pants.

She grinned wickedly up at him, undoing the buttons. "Remember the last time I was like this?"

"Fuck. Yes. The image of you, down on your knees, your mouth around me, was going to keep me sane for centuries."

His eyes darkened as he watched her shove his pants down around his knees and take his massive length in her hand. Idly running her hand from base to tip, she enjoyed his reaction.

"You like this?" She ran her tongue along the same path her hand had just taken.

"Yes," he grunted, his hands tightening in her hair.

"How about this?" She ran one fang along an engorged vein that lined his shaft.

"Especially that," he rasped.

Using the sharp tip of that fang, she nicked the vein just enough for a drop to leak out.

Rhys jerked, his breath leaving in a rush. "Do it again."

She complied and he jerked a second time. Then she licked the wounds closed and took him as far as she could into her mouth.

Rhys groaned and let his head drop back. "That mouth of yours is heaven."

She tried not to smile as she sucked up and down his length, swirling her tongue along the way.

When his hips thrust with her motion, she knew he was close. Increasing the pressure and speed, she worked him into an explosion.

With a roar, Rhys went rigid, only his hips wrenching back and forth as he spilled into her mouth. She kept up her ministrations until he was well spent, his taste just as addicting as his blood.

Before she thought he had recovered, he was drawing her to her feet.

"My turn to taste you," he growled, kicking his pants off the rest of the way. His mouth captured hers and he ripped her pants apart as he devoured her lips.

He lifted her and carried her to into the kitchen. Setting her butt down on the table, he snagged a chair behind him with his foot and broke off the kiss to sit down.

She waited for Rhys to make the first move. It was much more erotic to give up that little bit of control.

He looked deep into her eyes as he spread her knees apart. Then his eyes dropped to her center.

"Perfect." He licked his lips and lifted her feet to his shoulders. Meeting her eyes one last time, giving her a chance to put a stop to his actions, he brought his attention back to her throbbing core.

Blowing softly as he leaned down, X almost collapsed back. It was just air, but she was on fire and the cooling breath was damn near orgasmic.

At least she thought so until his tongue delved in, licking her from core to clit. X did collapse back, but only onto her elbows. She wanted to watch everything the male was doing to her, wanted to see the titillating view of his head buried between her legs.

She was spread out on his table, the main course, as he tasted and licked. She even surprised herself when she cried out as he nibbled on her sensitive nub. He didn't use his hands, keeping them wrapped tightly around her thighs. Only his tongue touched her center, licking, rolling and flicking over her clitoris until she arched up, shoving herself against him, her head flung back. She cried his name over and over again, hollering a "yes" in between each time. Her legs quivered, but he was relentless, didn't let up until she reached her climax and went hurtling over the edge. He continued on, wringing every drop of pleasure out of her.

The world went blank even though X's eyes were wide open. Usually, she retreated to a dark corner in her mind, letting her body do what nature had cursed it with, but not this time. No, she was present, she *wanted* it, she *wanted* the male who was settled between her thighs. She *wanted* him to keep going. She had never wanted and she wanted everything now.

Another orgasm quickly approached. Rhys shifted his head, the new angle launching her into another explosive release.

She couldn't even call his name, only scream her pleasure, the sound bouncing off the walls.

Abruptly, Rhys stood, her legs slipping off his shoulders, only for him to catch them and wrap them around his waist as he pulled her up against him. X was damn near boneless, but she wrapped her arms around his shoulders and hung on as he lifted and carried her through the cabin into his bedroom.

The thought of soon feeling this male inside of her stoked the furnace raging within. After two of the most powerful orgasms in history, she should be spent. But she would never get enough of Rhys Fitzsimmons.

He climbed up onto the bed and held her to him as he laid her down and stretched out over her.

Even in her dizzying state, his heavy body on top of her shorted out her common sense and images of her first two years at Sigma shot through her head.

X gasped, her head jerking back against the mattress, her body going stiff.

Rhys rose to his elbows, nothing but concern on his face. When he saw her panicked expression, he untangled her legs and pushed off to the side, but didn't leave the bed.

"I'm sorry," he said immediately.

X's chest heaved as she managed to get her breathing under control. Why the fuck would she have a panic attack now? She was with someone she respected deeply, had the hots for, and she wanted to be with him, in every sense of the word.

She had never lost her head over what happened to her.

"No, it's not you." She drew her hands down her face, then gave up and threw an arm over her eyes. She shouldn't feel humiliated but she did. "I don't get it. I've never had that reaction."

"Is it because I'm special?" She heard the subtle teasing in his voice, trying to lighten the mood.

"After my conditioning," bitterness dripped off that last word, "I made sure it was always just about fucking, and I was always in control, even when I mentally checked out. I guess the feel of a male pinning me down surfaced a lot of memories." X lifted her arm and rolled to her side, facing him. "Are you bitter? That I was with others, but I can't deal being with you right now?"

"No," he said emphatically. "Sigma ruined the act of sex for you, made it into a tool, a weapon."

So. True. "I used that weapon a lot," she admitted quietly.

"Alex, you're only thirty years old. I've been around a few centuries. It's safe to say my bed count is higher than yours. Do you hold that against me?" When she shook her head, he continued, "Your history only matters to me because it's your history. I hold no blame toward you, only toward those who hurt you."

"You're a good guy, you know that?" Tracing his face with a finger, they lay there for several minutes facing each other. Out of the blue, her stomach rumbled.

His lips quirked. "Want to help me make supper?"

***

X flowed gracefully to her feet to not disturb the sleeping male. After they had made supper and eaten, engaging in forced small talk, he curled up with her in bed, ready to protect her sleep. In a role reversal, Rhys had fallen asleep while she lay awake thinking. She had figured out what she needed.

Stooping down to grab her shirt, she noiselessly dressed. Then she grabbed the bag the Guardians had packed for her that she had never unpacked. When she was done with something, she had always returned it back to the bag. A giant clue she wasn't ready to settle in. She made it to the door of the bedroom when she stopped.

Come on. I've never been chicken shit in my life.

Turning back, she faced the large male passed out on the bed.

"Rhys."

His eyes opened straight on her, and he sat up, his expression circumspect.

"I've gotta go." *Good one. Way to explain the shit going on in your head.*

His brows drew down, waiting for her to continue.

"I was just so young, you know?" She adjusted the duffel to fling it over her shoulder. "I need to be alone with myself for a while. Learn what this hot mess is all about. The last twelve years were about survival. I can't go straight from being Agent X to being your mate. I need some time."

Rhys exhaled slowly, his powerful shoulders slumping. "You know I'll give you all the time you need."

"I know," she said quietly. "You're the most amazing male, like, ever. I need to learn how to be Alex King before I can be E's friend, or Sarah and Ron's aunt, or…your mate."

"I understand."

"And…I need you to stay out of my dreams. I can't repay you for your years of protection, but I need to face them now."

He leveled his gaze on her. "I'll stay away."

She paused again. "Thanks." Fuck, that sounded lame.

He lifted his chin toward the hook by the door. "Take my car. There's some cash in the glove box if you need it."

"I have a stash, too. I was going to hoof it, but," she snagged the keys off the wall, "a drive sounds nice." A radio sounded even nicer.

She gave him a small smile, mostly as an apology, before she left to find the car. He didn't have to tell her how to get to it. She could find the garage and get the car, or she'd just boost one of the other ones instead.

Swiftly making her way down to the lodge and into the garage, she didn't run across anyone. There was a plethora of nondescript dark sedans to choose from, so she hit the unlock button and found the one that was his.

Climbing in, she groaned. It smelled like Rhys; all piney and virile male. His scent was comforting and heartbreaking at the same time. Ignoring the hurt in her chest, she jammed the keys in and started the car.

She made it out to the main road with no interference. The other Guardians wouldn't be pleased when they realized she had left. Mercury and Bennett didn't really trust her and wouldn't want her roaming freely.

Then there was the council. What would happen when they found out about her? She should stay and face them, make her presence known to all shifter and vampire kind. So if she "mysteriously" died, everyone would know one of the councils was behind it.

While Madame G may have been cruel and evil, X was sure she wasn't as underhanded and devious as the Lycan Council could be. The Vampire Council, too, but they were busy with Demetrius' revolt.

Aiming the car away from West Creek, X drove into the darkness.

Chapter Eight

X didn't have to consult a map. She had
known the way by heart. This was her first
real stop after leaving Rhys behind. She
maneuvered on the winding, desolate road, until she
neared the area.

Pulling off the side of the road, memories
assaulted her. Oh, the nightmares she'd have once
she fell asleep after this. She got out of the car after
killing the engine, and eyed the barren stretch of
road that meandered its way down the side of a
mountain. It plugged up so badly in the winter that
once the mine went dry no one was interested in
battling the elements to settle anywhere on the
stretch of mountain that the road served.

It had been a favorite area for her parents to go
at dusk. Once the sun settled deep below the
horizon, her mom would hop out, and X and her dad
would shift. They'd just run and be free.

Fog drifted away from her mouth with each
exhale. The temperature was chilly in town, but it
was even colder on the mountain. It smelled like it
might snow.

With resignation, X trekked down the steep side of the road where the Agents had shoved her parent's car after burning the bodies within.

It was precipitous, the land rugged. She even put her boots on for the trek. It wasn't long before she smelled the rusted metal where the mangled car had struck a tree and stopped in its forever resting place. The accident wouldn't have been visible from any stretch of the road. The Agents had chosen their attack position well.

Off to the right of the hunk of metal were three mounds where the earth had been disturbed, three makeshift graves. She presumed her brother, after searching for his family, found the horrific scene and laid them to rest.

X sat next to the graves, silently considering the person she used to be, the mourning she had never gotten to do. A hot tear burned a path down her cheek, followed by another, until they cascaded constantly. Gah, when was the last time she cried?

She sat for hours, knowing it was only the beginning of her healing journey. Once she left, it was just her and she would have to open up her mind and deal with everything she had buried inside. It was so tempting just to keep it all shoved into a dark corner of her brain. One thing she had learned the last few days was that it wouldn't give her the life she wanted if she did that. She deserved more; Rhys deserved more.

With a long inhale, X stood and gave the lonely graves one last look before she headed back to the car.

***

Boss, we have serious company. Mercury's voice floated through Rhys' mind.

Rhys didn't have to ask. He had a strong suspicion what kind of shit had just dropped on his doorstep.

Are they in the lodge?

They barged in through the damn door. I told Dani to stay put, I don't want any of those bastards around her.

If the council was really undermining human mates, then Dani and Cassie needed to stay as far away as possible. And if the rumors about the council assassinating Mercury's colony had any substance, it wasn't a good idea for Mercury to be standing in front of them, gathering attention.

Are you with them?

Yeah. Bennett's smooth-talking them.

Good. Bennett could still turn on the charm when he needed to.

Be right there.

Rhys left his office and strode down to the lodge's entryway. All he could hope for was that his pack wouldn't suffer for his actions.

Waiting just inside the door of the lodge, with Mercury and Bennett, were four shifters. Rhys recognized one as Malcolm and Harrison's father. The other three carried the scent unique to a Guardian and must be from the council's personal pack. There were two males and one female Guardian.

"Councilman Wallace." Rhys addressed the stately shifter who carried a heavy air of arrogance.

"Commander Fitzsimmons," he acknowledged. "Where's the hybrid?"

Displeasure rippled through Rhys. They treated X as if she was an object. Constantly referring to her as an Agent was better than "the hybrid."

She was *his* hybrid. "Let's move to my office," Rhys suggested.

The three burly guards shifted, a clear sign that they didn't want to get left out of the talks.

"Only if the hybrid is in your office," Councilman Wallace replied smoothly.

"The *hybrid* has a name."

One of the council's Guardians made a derogatory noise. "She has a letter."

Rhys' body stiffened at the insult. Mercury and Bennett tensed, ready to back him up. He glared at the strange shifter until the male dropped his gaze. "X. Call her X."

Councilman Wallace narrowed his sharp whiskey eyes on Rhys. "And where is X?"

When Rhys came to terms, all those years ago, that his mate was an Agent, he knew it would eventually come to this. That was even before he learned of her dual heritage. After that, it was only a matter of time, and he'd bought as much he could afford. It was time to pay up.

"She's gone."

Now it was the council's Guardians who tensed. No doubt they expected a confrontation and had come ready for an altercation with the infamous hybrid.

To his credit, Councilman Wallace didn't appear very surprised. "Explain."

"I let her go." Rhys hoped they didn't smell a lie. Of course Rhys didn't *let* X do anything. "She needed to figure things out after the trauma she's been through, and she couldn't do it here. Not with the council breathing down her neck."

It was a weak attempt at laying the blame at the council's feet, but Rhys felt like being a dick.

The shrewd councilman studied him. "You do realize that all who knew about this are subject to disciplinary action."

"The others didn't know I let her leave."

"How long has she been gone?"

"Five days."

Councilman Wallace expelled a heavy sigh. Rhys almost believed the male wasn't looking forward to carrying out his duty punishing Rhys or his pack.

"Five days. Yet neither you, nor any of your team, reported her absence?"

"They wouldn't have." Time to let the bomb drop. "She's my mate."

The councilman's eyes widened, and his guards shook their heads in disbelief. Rhys sensed nothing from Mercury and Bennett behind him. They were passively watching the exchange. He had discussed several scenarios with them about how all this could play out, and they waited to see what happened.

"Well," the councilman drawled, "at least she's the mate of one of ours and not of a vampire. That solves one problem." He regarded Rhys. "Are you saying the other Guardians were respecting your right to protect your mate as you see fit?"

"Yes." Now that was interesting. It was almost as if the councilman was leading him into answering in a way that would be beneficial to Rhys' pack. If his team was following pack rules of protecting mates, then the blame would lie solely on Rhys. Otherwise, Councilman Wallace could take them all in to face a tribunal.

"Is your mating official? Have you been through the ceremony?" The councilman's nostrils flared, likely trying to sense if Rhys had been at least marked yet by his mate.

"You can understand, it's a delicate situation."

"The council will hunt her," Councilman Wallace warned.

Mercury grunted behind him. "Good luck."

"I agree," the councilman replied, congenially. "If I didn't have such a difficult mate myself, I might not sympathize."

Rhys had learned the twins' mom was a vicious female. The males themselves told him that with a sense of both mortification and pride.

Councilman Wallace beckoned his guards forward. "Regardless, we will have to bring you in, and the other former Agent, E."

"I understand. And Agent E and his family left yesterday."

Rhys heard rumbles from the council's Guardians, obviously not happy.

Councilman Wallace exhaled a long-suffering sigh, even rolling his eyes. "Again, no one reported it?"

"It's not unusual for them to go to town on a family excursion." They'd only ever done so once, before they left for an indefinite amount of time a day ago. "I wasn't going to declare them officially missing until they were gone a full forty-eight hours."

"What a nice head start," Councilman Wallace said dryly. "You will come along willingly?"

The other Guardians shifted cautiously while Mercury and Bennett appeared relaxed. They were anything but.

Rhys nodded. "Of course. Bennett Young will resume command of the pack."

The councilman studied Rhys closely before turning his attention to a tightly controlled Bennett. "Unless we discover he's keeping information from us as well."

The male lifted a questioning eyebrow at Bennett, who gazed impassively back before replying, "I will command loyally in Commander Fitzsimmons' place until he is reestablished as pack leader."

A humorous glint entered Councilman Wallace's eyes, as if he caught the subversive way Bennett avoided his veiled accusation.

"Hand over your weapons, Commander," the female Guardian demanded.

Resigned, Rhys stripped himself of every piece of metal he was wearing. Instead of tossing them to the stout brunette, he passed them back to Mercury.

He saw one of the council Guardian's lips curl up in a sneer at the show of defiance.

"Commander Fitzsimmons," the councilman announced, "with the authority of the Lycan Council, I must strip you of title—"

"Temporarily," Bennett interrupted. The sneering Guardian growled at the interruption of their distinguished guest.

Perhaps Councilman Wallace was offended, but he only appeared more amused. "*Possibly* temporarily strip you of title as West Creek Guardian Commander." He peered past Rhys to study the new commander. "Bennett Young, by the power of the Lycan Council, I grant you the title of West Creek Guardian Commander."

"Temporarily," Bennett said in affirmation.

More amusement highlighted the councilman's eyes. "*Possibly* temporary."

"Good enough," Bennett said as he nodded.

Councilman Wallace's face grew serious. "Let's go."

Chapter Nine

X trotted through the pines, her paws padding agilely through the light snow. It was freaking gorgeous here. Her breath huffed, and she even let her tongue loll out.

The sun was setting, and she would soon have to find shelter for the night. If she was in human form she'd be pretty damn cold, and…She sighed in resignation.

How spoiled she'd been with Rhys protecting her dreams. It was bad enough living with the memories. But the dreams—no, nightmares…Even sleeping in her wolf form, she'd awaken with a start, snarling at the darkness. They were brutal and devastatingly accurate. It was like reliving her conditioning and training all over again. The vampires and Agents who had played with her like she was the latest toy revisited her. They looked the same, smelled the same. The fangs that drew from her vein as she strained to tune out her biology under another's body, helpless against the pain disguised as pleasure coursing through her body.

For years, she cursed her genetics. Hated that something she had despised doing had to feel good, end in orgasm. At least now she knew it only merely felt good physically. What she had experienced with Rhys before she left was phenomenal. Her mind was emotionally connected to the male, her body experienced nothing short of ecstasy, and she had *almost* felt complete.

If she could bring herself to mate the big lug, then that sense of completion would only heighten any physical relations between them. As it was, they didn't even have to be touching for her to get electrified when he walked into the room. Every nerve in her body yearned to get closer to the imposing shifter in hopes that maybe her skin would feel the stroke of his.

Gah! She hated feeling like she needed him. This little "I need to find myself" mission wouldn't work if she pined away in the pines for Rhys Fitzsimmons.

She'd been gone almost two months. Winter was settling in around the country, especially in the mountains. After visiting the place where it all started, she drove to where she used to run with her family. Thought it would be a fitting place to start.

Finding a nice, desolate area, she had trudged deep into the evergreens and stripped down. But she couldn't shift. Her memories were assaulting her, and they were good ones for a change. That made it all the harder.

So she's wove her way back to the car, took a siesta, and drove to somewhere she'd never been before. It took days. She and E had covered quite the territory for Sigma, and she knew exactly where all the shifter colonies were situated deep in the woods. Once she had found a spot away from paranormals and humans alike, she left the car and her clothing and became a large black wolf with brilliant green eyes.

In the mountains, she had to rely on her senses and instincts, not cunning and deception. It was refreshing. Her senses were still being used for survival, but in a good, clean way. That became her routine for the next few weeks. Drive, have a look-see, strip, and run. Sometimes for days. Head back to the car, repeat.

But the nightmares…Every night, every damn time she closed her eyes, they were there. Reminding her of everything she had been through, all of the people who had suffered along with her. Every night, she jerked awake snarling, screaming if she was in human form.

She was tired. So she ran more.

***

Month Three

It was that time of the week.

The massive shifter loomed over him, a meaty fist caught him in the jaw. Rhys' head flung to the side and then rolled back. He let it hang there. It was a small reprieve, but if he brought it up, sometimes Mastiff hit him again without pause.

Mastiff fit his name—big head, burly body. He wasn't nearly as cute as the full canine variety and he was a whole lot meaner. With a skull buzz and wearing a wife-beater, he looked as mean as he really was.

Rhys brought his head up and, as per their normal routine, he spit blood at the determined male. This, of course, earned him another fist to the cheekbone. The familiar, refreshingly painful crack of bone seared through his face as his head whipped to the side.

The council sent Mastiff to interrogate Rhys via his beefy hooks. Rhys didn't break, Mastiff had a good time, all ended well. By now, the council knew Rhys wouldn't offer information on X. Rhys had been so tight lipped, they didn't suspect that he knew who X's entire family was, where they resided, or that two of them were part of his pack. They weren't even sure she had any living relatives.

The last part made him smile. Which pissed off Mastiff, who aimed his next punch at Rhys' gut.

Air whooshed out as Rhys doubled over as much as possible, being tied into a metal chair, his hands bound behind the back of it. It felt like his stomach was going to come out his throat. Coughing and gagging, Rhys righted himself.

"Mastiff," he wheezed, "you can do better than that."

Mastiff's pudgy lips thinned. "I will do much better if you don't contact your female." His voice rumbled through the room.

"Fuck. Do you gargle with rocks in the morning?" Rhys had been dreaming about his mate too much. He usually wasn't so flippant. "Hit me again, big guy."

The barrel-chested male's mouth twitched. He heaved his mighty fist back. For fun, Rhys took bets on where the devastating blow was going to land.

Ten bucks on the face.

Gut. Rhys heaved forward, lost for breath. It was the gut.

Mastiff grabbed Rhys' face and jerked it up. Rhys could smell the bacon the male had eaten for breakfast. His own stomach would've rumbled if it wasn't in excruciating pain. All he had gotten to eat in his private cell was cheap shit: oatmeal, canned meat product, and disintegrating vegetable matter.

The personal punisher of the council finished whaling on Rhys. Then he unhooked Rhys from his chair, leaving his hands behind his back, and towed him back to his cell. Once inside, Rhys assumed the position as Mastiff closed and locked the door. Putting his cuffed hands against the slot in the door, the shackles fell away, and Mastiff yanked them out completely.

Taking a page from X's book, because damn it was fun, he called through the door. "Until next time, Bulldog."

Mastiff growled and slammed the door with his fist, making it shudder. Rhys chuckled and stabbing pain shot through his ribs. He collapsed on the ungodly uncomfortable cot in the room for some healing rest.

At first, Rhys was surprised they kept him in a private cell, away from the other prisoners. He initially suspected it was to drive him crazy, being alone for months, but it seemed like there was another reason. He never interacted with other prisoners, was never hauled through the cells as a show of force, never passed by anyone getting dragged down the hallway to and from his weekly interrogation.

It couldn't be just because they were trying to drive him to such boredom that he'd break down and contact X, luring her to the council's location so they could trap her.

He wasn't tempted. Ever. What he was experiencing was nothing compared to what she was recovering from. He would give her time, and entertain the thought that she might come back to him someday. Some year. He'd waited this long, he was willing to wait longer.

If the council sought to drive him feral from forced isolation, they couldn't be more wrong. Yes, he was an unmated male in his prime. He'd gone longer than most, keeping his sanity without a mating bond. At first it was duty, pure and simple. He lived for his work. Then he laid eyes on X, and that was all he needed. Now, he had no worries.

Years and years could go by, he wouldn't forget the taste of his mate on his tongue, the cries of his name coming from her lips as she came from his touch.

At night, when he wouldn't dream of that—and he dreamed of it often—he walked the dreams of those around council headquarters. He found out a lot of secrets, but nothing that could help his pack implicate the council in any wrongdoing. Or at least any wrongdoing regarding plotting against human mates or packs with special skills. That meant either there was nothing nefarious to discover or only certain council members were involved.

He figured it was the latter. It had to be. The council didn't know of his power, thought it was something more mental, like X's hypnosis or Jace's power of persuasion. But the five males on the Lycan Council didn't get to where they were by being weak. Rhys needed to tread carefully around their dreams, so they wouldn't sense his presence and figure out a way to keep him from doing it.

So far, in the almost three months he'd been incarcerated, he had made it into the minds of two of the newer council members. Councilman Demke and Councilman Ute had both been members for about fifty years. They were charged with Lycan education and tradition, helping isolated colonies carry out council policies. Rhys had no reason to think either male was involved in underhanded plans against their own kind. Their dreams only showed him how traditional some packs were in their pack mentality.

Two nights ago, however, Rhys had a major victory, sneaking his way into Councilman Wallace's dreams. He found nothing of use, but he found a whole lot that was interesting. The male dreamed of another female, one with oak-colored hair like the councilman's sons, Malcolm and Harrison. The female looked nothing like the councilman's mate, who Rhys had met only once.

Once was enough. She mastered the fine art of emasculating males. And females, if possible.

After he recovered from the beating, Rhys would walk the male's dreams again. Then he would hover around the dreams of Councilman Seether and Hargrath. The twin's father had only been a member of the council for a century, but the other two were much older, and had been members as long as Rhys was old. They probably traced their direct ancestors to the ancients, the most powerful, pure-blooded shifters. It would make sense if they were behind any attempts at eradicating human mates.

In the meantime, he could explore the rest of the compound. He had also popped in and out of the dreams of the council's Guardian pack. Many of them were new, but Rhys suspected at least one, probably more, were carrying out orders to harm human mates.

He tried to walk the dreams of the other prisoners but, weird thing was, he couldn't find them. Like there was some kind of barrier around the rest of the prison. Was it so the prisoners couldn't get any messages out using mental abilities? Or so outsiders wouldn't know what kind of prisoners were being held?

Heal first. Dream walk later.

***

That. Is a really big. Bear.

For the last three months, X had avoided civilization and her own kind. She'd come across all kinds of other wildlife, but, hello—she was top of the food chain.

As much as she missed Rhys' blood, and she *missed* his blood, she was making do with her wildlife kills. Rabbit blood didn't get her very far, but every so often she'd take down a deer.

She almost got a rack of antlers in the ass from the one buck she had come across. Maybe she'd gotten a little cocky with that target. But she'd been hungry, she missed cheesecake, and she could swear she heard the creature's powerful blood surging through his veins, hyped on adrenaline from the chase she gave.

He put up an admirable fight, but in the end she won. Out of respect, she dined on him for as long as possible, the cold weather preventing him from turning bad. Once she had left, the scavengers quickly took over.

The bear she was facing now, however, was not below her in the food chain. He was groggy and out looking for food as it had been a mild week for winter weather. The big brown bear must've taken a pause in hibernation to obtain more fuel. Her father had told her they could do that; made sure she was up on moody bear behavior before he let her go running her wolf alone.

X's heart rate spiked as the bear huffed and dipped his head, sniffing at her. When he swaggered forward, his flanks heaving, she danced back. They went on like that for several seconds before she decided to turn tail and run.

Darting around trees, she paused to glance back after several yards.

The bear couldn't have cared less. He foraged, pawing through the snow for vegetation.

X was…disappointed. A little chase would've been a nice distraction.

Not that she was bored.

Okay, she was bored. Maybe that was a sign she needed to start interacting with people.

That thought didn't dismay her as much as usual. Previously, the thought of roaming through town and acting "normal" felt like too onerous of a task. Not to mention she had to dodge anything with fangs while she was out and about.

Now, it seemed less daunting. Less trying to blend in and not evaluate everyone in the room. Not having to interact with people because they were targets, or that she was trying to get information out of them. She felt less pressure to become a proper shifter's mate, even if the only pressure came from within.

As she trotted away from the disappointedly non-confrontational bear, she thought about how the nightmares had lessened. They didn't plague her sleep every night. More often, she began dreaming of the good times, of the first eighteen years of her life. And that last night before she had left the lodge. That dream woke her up in a sweat, but for a much different reason than her nightmares.

Gawd, Rhys and his tongue were phenomenal.

Before she entered society again and learned how to play nice, she would have to visit her brother. *That* she was putting off. But she was getting closer to being ready.

Maybe.

Chapter Ten

Month Four

"**A**re you doing okay, ma'am?" the young saleslady asked in a high-pitched drawl.

"Hella good." *Now leave me the fuck alone.*

Trying to decide one's own personal style was a sort of torturous fun. It was easier when her daily choices were black on black. For fun, she used to tie on a corset. She'd had clothes for the clubs and she had jeans and T-shirts with witty sayings. Right now, she was looking for clothes that Alex King would wear.

Alex liked her shirts, and her corsets, and her short club dresses, but they were so X. She was on a damn personal journey, had spent the last few months in fur on four legs, and she needed some new shit.

"Is there any other size I can get you?" The saleslady buzzed like a fly around her changing room. Did she get commission or something?

Alex whipped open the dressing room door, wearing only her lacy fire-engine red bra and panties, with denim leggings pulled halfway up her thighs. Good thing for the sales associate, Alex had decided to give the whole underwear thing a try.

The petite young girl squeaked and jumped back, her eyes wide.

"As you can see, I haven't gotten that far." Alex gave a sassy smile and cocked her head. "How 'bout if I need anything, I'll let you know?"

The little blonde's eyes were stuck on Alex's ample breasts, then her toned six-pack, then back up to her eyes. "Oh yes." She flushed red. "I'm sorry."

"Just doin' your job. I get it." Alex closed the door and finished trying on the articles of clothing she had picked out.

Leggings were a wonderful thing. Too bad they didn't do shit to stop a knife, but shopping today was not about tactical gear, so a few would make her purchase list. Along with those boots she passed in the window on her way in. Those boots were fi-yah!

Checking out her image, Alex pondered her hair. It had grown a couple of inches since she last took to it with her clippers. It wasn't shaggy as much as irritating, it hung in her eyes.

She moved her bangs around, fluffed up the back. Maybe a little taper around her neck and sides, a little layer and texture to the rest. Alex King was going to get a new 'do.

***

Councilman Wallace waited for Rhys' answer. He had appeared at Rhys' cell door, looking oddly casual in khakis and a maroon button-down. He wore no tie, but left the top button of his shirt open to display a hint of the muscle that lay underneath. Rhys guessed the male was similar to him in age.

"Maybe," Rhys answered.

"That's your best guess?" The councilman had asked Rhys if he thought X would ever come for him.

"Not gonna lie."

The male cocked his head. "I can see why my boys respect you." His voice dropped so low only Rhys could hear. "I can see why they were willing to spy on dear ol' dad for you."

Rhys hid his surprise. He had sent Malcolm and Harrison to spy on the council because of who their dad was. "They tell you?"

Councilman Wallace scoffed. "I knew they didn't come home for a long visit because they missed me. Definitely not for their mother." He shrugged, his hands resting in his pockets, his voice still low. "After your Guardian was killed and they arrived here, I figured you had become suspicious."

"What would I be suspicious of?"

The male gave him a mysterious smile. "I trust you to do your job, Fitzsimmons. I would be of little use to our species deceased and that's what will happen if I speak about my own suspicions."

"It's pretty hard to do my job in here."

Rhys got a wan smile in return.

"Is it? I'm sure Commander Young is picking up where you left off." Councilman Wallace peered closely at him. "I'm sure you've found a way to keep yourself busy?"

"I don't know what you're talking about." Shit. Had he been too abrupt in a dream and gotten noticed?

Sadness crept into the male's eyes. "Don't worry. It took me a while to figure it out. I have that dream every night, of my sweet Camille. She's the reason my mate is so mean." At the look on Rhys' face, some amusement crept in. "No, Fitzsimmons. Camille was my daughter, older sister to the twins. I've dreamt of her every day since she was killed. So you see, when I felt something off…"

Damn.

"Tread carefully, Commander." The fact that the councilman just referred to him by that title spoke volumes. "But you're on the right track."

***

Month Five

Nerves were getting to her. She had memorized the address, figured they hadn't moved on, hoped they did, prayed they hadn't.

Brushing her hair off her face, she couldn't imagine what John would think when he opened the door. She needed to do this. Needed to face this demon. Her brother wasn't a demon. Far from it. There had been such a large gap in age between them, he had almost been like a father figure, or a favored uncle. He had doted on her, and she had lived for when he would bring his mate, Kenna, by with the kids. How would he act now, after he knew about everything she'd been through, what she'd done?

"You can knock." She whipped around to the familiar voice behind her. A tall, dark form strode out from the trees. "I doubt Kenna knows you're here yet."

Kenna was human; even her heightened senses from mating John wouldn't be good enough to sense Alex. John's shouldn't be, either, unless he'd been keeping them sharp over the years.

"John." Good one. Twelve years since she's seen him and that was all she could say?

He kept moving toward her, his green eyes, a deeper green than her own, reflected like the predator he was. "I'm glad you came."

"Are you?" After the phone call, she wasn't sure how he felt.

Her chest tightened with suspense as the tall figure of her brother came closer. He looked just like she remembered him, a few inches taller than her, with hair a shade darker than his daughter's. His hands were shoved into the pockets of his pants, his feet were bare.

"Alexandria." Her name came on a breath, like he'd been told she was alive but it had been too hard to believe until he saw her.

"Yep."

He shook his head. "Sarah said you'd left and I hoped maybe you'd come here." A wry smile curved his lips. "I headed straight to where Mom and Dad were buried, but I sensed I had already missed you."

She smiled despite herself. "I wasn't sure you wanted to see me."

A tortured frown creased his brow. "Of course I want to see you." He moved closer, hesitantly, like she might run away. "You have to understand my shock when you called. It was like a dream come true. But honestly, I have horrible survivor's guilt. The remains were burned pretty badly, but I should've known that wasn't you. I should've searched for you."

"No," she said adamantly. "You had two kids to raise and protect."

They both stood unmoving, and she was sure he was thinking about the what-ifs and what-might-have-beens just as she.

"Want to head inside?"

Alex smiled. "Yeah. I'd like that."

***

After Councilman Wallace informed Rhys he had sensed him in his dreams, Rhys decided he needed to back off from the other two councilmen he hadn't yet attempted to dream walk on. They were older and more powerful than both Wallace and Rhys. Councilman Seether and Councilman Hargrath would have to wait.

Mastiff's dreams were fairly easy to get into. The burly Guardian who had been pummeling the shit out of Rhys for months may have also been assigned to interrogate other prisoners.

Rhys hovered at the edges. He saw random scatterings of thought. Mastiff hadn't settled into a deep sleep yet so Rhys could give him mental nudges. Using his powers, he sent dream suggestions into Mastiff's mind to recall his sessions with other prisoners.

It was only moments before Rhys could see flickers of shifters' faces. He could see them how Mastiff had seen them when he was torturing them. Mastiff was a one trick pony; he used his fists to do his dirty work.

Suddenly a scene unfolded before Rhys. Councilman Seether was speaking privately to Mastiff, and in the next instant, the scene turned into Mastiff busting into a house, grabbing a young human woman and—

Rhys flinched and the scene went black. He opened his eyes to find himself awake in his cell, which meant Mastiff had woken up. The dream obviously bothered even the cruel shifter. The human woman hadn't stood a chance.

Trying to drift back to sleep, Rhys realized he wouldn't have to walk the dreams of Seether and Hargrath. He could hunt what he needed of the two councilmen out of others' dreams.

***

Month Six

"And who will this be for?" the petite barista asked.

"Alex."

"Okay," she said perkily, "we'll have it right out to you."

Alex wandered to the edge of the coffee shop to wait for her venti latte. She picked up a complimentary newspaper to look over while waiting.

After her visit with John and Kenna, she had stayed in cheap motels and started interacting with people. The hours she'd spent with her brother and his wife had revitalized her. It wasn't until they had welcomed her in with complete acceptance despite her frank honesty about the past twelve years that she'd realized how much their possible rejection had bogged her mental healing down. The only negative emotion she'd sensed from them matched the sadness she felt for the years lost to them.

Without Rhys' blood, and being unable and unwilling to feed from another, she started socializing in the evenings so the sun wouldn't take its toll on her vampire half. Her blood need wasn't as great when she stayed in shifter form, but wandering on two legs would make her thirsty for more than coffee.

Roaming the woods and mountains, she had to make sure she chose towns with a low shifter and vampire ratio. Although she'd probably smell like a shifter after being in wolf form so often, she didn't want to chance an encounter. Who knew what had gone on while she was away.

Her name was called, her new name, her *real* name. She grabbed her coffee and walked out to the sidewalk. Taking a sip, she wandered until she reached a gap between the buildings that led to an alley. Turning casually into the alley, she headed toward the giant parking ramp that lined half the block. When she cleared a brick office building, she stepped behind it.

A quiet scraping of footsteps from the direction she had come drew nearer. They approached where she waited, rushing toward the parking ramp.

A male scurried past and she slipped in behind him. With the arm that wasn't holding her coffee, she circled the male around the neck and yanked him behind the building.

He grunted and struggled. She kneed him in between the legs while she kept an iron grip around his neck. He groaned and tried to drop down, his hands releasing Alex's arm to cup his balls.

She wedged her knee between his legs again and he went still.

"Why are you following me?" she asked casually, taking a sip from her coffee. She had smelled two male shifters following her when she reached the coffee shop, but she had wanted her damn coffee first.

Easing just enough pressure so he could speak, he gasped, "Reward."

Oooh, how much was she worth?

"Who's offering the reward?"

He lurched and twisted, reaching between them to grab the gun he had hidden in his waistband. Only, when Alex shoved him away, she had his gun and was pointing it directly at him.

She took another casual sip of coffee; her aim remained rock steady. The male froze, hands in the air.

She waived the gun at him to let him know she was waiting for an answer.

"The council. They're offering ten-thousand dollars to whoever can turn you in."

Alex snorted. "They thought someone could turn me in?" The male took a nervous inhale. She waved the gun at him again. "Go on. How long has this reward been offered?"

"F-for a couple months. They couldn't get her mate, uh, your mate, to turn you in."

Alex's blood ran cold. The council has Rhys?

She leveled her blazing gaze on him, catching his frightened brown eyes in her hypnotic stare. "Tell me everything you know about me and my mate."

"He's some Guardian from up north. The council is holding him to lure you in. When that didn't work, they released your description to all the packs, offering a reward for information on your whereabouts."

"And you thought you'd be tough enough to bring me in?" A touch of humor laced her voice. He was a scrawny pup, barely old enough to drink.

"I was going to knock you out so when my friend brought the car around, we could put you in the trunk."

"Shitty plan, you know that, right?"

He looked sheepish, even under her hypnotic hold. "I do now."

A car slowed at the alley's entrance. There was the doofus friend.

Increasing her concentration, she spoke quickly. "You lost me in the alley and dropped your gun. Call the council, tell them you had a sighting, but you can't be sure it was the right shifter."

His eyes went blank. The car was getting closer, the engine noise growing louder. The friend had turned into the alley and was creeping in their direction.

She released the young shifter from her hold, and when he turned to peak out from the behind the building, she made her exit.

By the time he looked back, he would only see his gun lying on the ground.

Chapter Eleven

Bennett rubbed his eyes and meandered toward the lodge to Commander Fitzsimmons' office. Scratch that, *his* office. But when this debacle was over, he'd gladly hand it back to Fitzsimmons.

Bennett had known the day would come when the pack would be his. Just not so soon. He'd rather be balls deep in Sarah's sweet body than pushing paperwork all night. Six months of this had felt like six years.

Fucking council. As if they didn't have enough to deal with, they had sent new recruits. "To make up for losing a Guardian," Councilman Seether said, as if they were a gift.

To spy on them, that was what Bennett and his pack thought. But they would play the game and keep Sarah and Ron's identity hidden, keep the location of E and his family hidden. Before their hand was forced, when they had finally revealed X was gone, Rhys and the Guardians met with E and made a plan. E, Ana, and Julio had left. None of the pack knew to where, it was safer for them that way.

They could reach E when necessary, using a burner phone like Sarah used with her parents. E had left willingly, but not without a, "you'd better fucking call me if you need me" warning. And yeah, when shit hit the fan, it would be nice to have a former Agent's expertise.

Bennett dragged his feet to the dreaded office. At least they didn't have the pain in the ass Sigma to deal with anymore. Demetrius and his devoted vampires had been leveling Sigma chapters all over. It was straight-up civil war on the down low for that species. It was old-world vampires who wanted to run anti-shifter organizations versus new-world vampires who wanted to form protection rings, much like the shifters had with their Guardians. That rankled the vampire elders even worse. Their species had always been about underground domination, not living in peace among humans and shifters.

The fact that X was protected by Demetrius took the former vampire rulers' focus off her status as a shifter's mate. Those old vamps would shit if they found out she had a brother, *and* he mated with a human, *and* he procreated.

Not just vampires would take issue, either. Many shifters would be dismayed that their blood was getting contaminated with vampire blood. Many others, though, would be relieved. Vampires mated to shifters were vampires who weren't looking to kill them.

Right now, Bennett had to get some training plans ready for the rookies who had arrived two months prior. The rookies showed up thinking they were ready to hit the field, typical young, dumb, and full of cum. Bennett snorted to himself. He would know. He had been that young male once.

Instead, Master Bellamy was putting them through some serious training regimens, proving to them that they were nowhere near ready. It also served to keep them busy, and too fatigued to snoop around and report back to the council. Hopefully.

Bennett sighed and inwardly cursed Rhys Fitzsimmons, even though he would do the same damn thing if he were in the male's shoes. Stepping into the office, he pulled up short.

Sitting at Fitzsimmons' desk, with her booted feet propped on top, hands behind her head, vivid green eyes alight with fierce determination, was the hybrid in question.

"X," Bennett said grimly.

"Actually, I prefer Alex." She swung her feet down and sat up. "Mind shutting the door." It wasn't a question.

Bennett scrubbed his tired face. His usual stony countenance was drawn with stress, his deep-blue eyes didn't carry their usual light.

He closed the door and collapsed in a chair across from the desk. Resting his cheek in one hand, elbow propped on the armrest, he stared wearily at her. "Do you know the shit-storm you've created?"

"It's totally my fault," she said sarcastically.

He waved her words off. "You know what I mean."

"I have one main question." She swept the hair off her forehead. She'd taken to styling it again, but to sneak not just into the lodge, but into Rhys' office, she'd had to get through some pretty tight spaces and it had gotten messed up. "Are we going to blow the lid on the council first or bust Rhys out first?"

Bennett huffed out a breath and reclined, his head on the back of the chair. "This pack is toast if we try to get Fitzsimmons out. The newbies the council sent us will either rat us out or be left in charge because the rest of us got dismissed."

"I can get Rhys out."

"Please. Not even you are that good."

"I'm sitting here, aren't I?"

Bennett flattened his lips at that. She knew she had made her point. It was her first time in the lodge. She couldn't have flashed into the office and no one had detected her presence at all.

"Malcolm and Harrison grew up around the council. They'd know the layout pretty well," he grudgingly offered.

"The less people who know I'm here, the better."

"Agreed." Bennett's expression was somber. "You can trust the twins. Sounds weird since their dad is on the council, but they're straight up. I'll let Mercury know, and the rest of the pack." His face twisted. "Except for the three rookies the council sent to spy on us. I trust you can keep out of sight?"

She studied Bennett. "Why are you being so helpful?"

"I'm a nice guy."

She rolled her eyes at him.

A small grin twisted his lips. "I didn't trust you, but not for the reasons I let on. I didn't want to be commander. I wanted to have more time with Sarah before I took over these duties. When you showed up, I had a feeling this is exactly where I'd land. Mates have a tendency to change our life's course, and as far as mates go, you're a doozey."

"Agreed," Alex echoed his statement from earlier. Then quietly she said, "I didn't want to hurt him."

"I don't think you did. Dude's a rock. Probably scared more than anything that you won't return for a century or two. Which would've been fine with me. By then I might've been ready to take on this dog and pony show. But the council took him instead, and here I am, an adult fucking babysitter for the council's spies."

"They're using him to bait me."

Bennett nodded in agreement.

"Well, if they want me, me is who they're going to get. I say we take down that bitch."

Bennett looked at her, not understanding her words at first. Then he gave his head a quick shake of disbelief because of the magnitude of what she proposed. "You aren't talking about the council are you?"

"Why wouldn't I be?"

"I agree, they're up to some bullshit. But the twins investigated for almost a year and came up with nada. They could barely even dig into anyone's business without being threatened to get kicked out. How are we going to take down the council without starting our own civil war?"

"I have connections your shifters don't."

"I'm sure you do." Bennett sighed, lost in thought. "If we do this, we have to time it right."

***

Alex aimed carefully down the hallway, then let the dart fly. It hit her target perfectly. The vampire slapped at his arm like he was swatting a mosquito. Only, by the time he looked down at the red-tipped dart sticking out from his sweater, he was slumping to the ground.

She smiled triumphantly to herself. Doc and his drugs were pretty damn awesome. The huge supply of drugs Madame G had designed had been destroyed. A mutual decision between Rhys and Demetrius after the compound had been taken over. As helpful as it'd be to study her concoctions, it was safer to have it all obliterated.

The shifters had been using their own tranqs for a while, and with Doc's help, they were refined for each species.

Alex trotted forward and wiggled the handle of the door. Locked of course, but a girl could hope. She searched the downed vampire's pockets and came up empty. Guess she'd have to enter the old-fashioned way.

She pulled the little kit from her belt and went to work on the lock. It was a standard lock, nothing digital. Everything else in the building had been, yet this room had a normal lock. The guard at the door was put in place instead of technology.

Bonus. It took longer to hack an electronically-secured door, and it was not as fun as knocking out a vampire.

The building itself was quite up-to-date, even though the outside looked like a crusty old warehouse that had fallen into disuse. The three floors below ground level were as modern as could be. The vampire in charge had spared no expense building the safe house.

Alex let herself in and dragged the vampire in behind her. The apartment was empty. After selecting a bottle of water from the fridge and having a seat on a barstool across from the door, she kept her tranq gun handy in case the guard started twitching. Alex crossed her legs, sipped some water, and waited.

Her timing tonight was crack on because she didn't have to wait long.

Demetrius opened the door. "Scurn, you in here using the head?"

As the tall vampire entered, he tripped over the massive guard lying unconscious in his entryway.

He reached for a weapon when Alex interrupted him. "Don't worry, it's just me."

Demetrius' head whipped up and he broke into a big grin. "X!"

She waved off her old name. "Alex."

He shut the door and strode to her. He was as devastatingly handsome as ever, and had already turned on his signature charm.

"Is that your real name?" He sat on the stool next to her, facing into the kitchen while she still faced toward the door.

"Close enough." She still needed to protect her family. Going around introducing herself as Alexandria King was a huge no-go.

"What can I do you for, Alex?" His voice had dropped a few notches into a seductive purr.

"I need some information."

A chuckle rumbled through his chest and she saw a fang flash as he smiled. "My pleasure, love."

"I'm looking for more of a collaboration than an exchange."

His grin broadened, his fangs gleaming. "We collaborate so well together."

Alex propped her elbow behind her on the bar and turned to face him. "I mean, just talking. You and me, clothes on."

He adopted a seductive pout, but when she didn't offer anything further, he sighed. "I knew that damn shifter would win out someday. Speaking of which," his nostrils flared, "I don't smell him on you. In fact, why didn't I scent you coming in?"

"Because I didn't want you to," she replied cryptically. She'd picked up her share of tricks working for Sigma for a decade.

"So you have mated him?"

"I didn't say that."

He looked at her, his pale-green eyes speculative. "The council has Fitzsimmons and they're offering a sizable reward for you. And you're here."

"Like you are doing with the Vampire Council, I think the Lycan Council needs a major overhaul."

"You realize when I win against our archaic government, I'll be in charge. You'd answer to me, hybrid."

"Like hell I'm going to answer to anyone."

Amusement was written across his face. "Unless you're going to form your own hybrid council, you need to come up with a proposal of how you, any kin of yours, *and* any future hybrids, should be treated by each species."

Dude had a point. She certainly wasn't going to form her own government. What. A. Headache.

"I'll give that point to you. Why don't you tell me what *your* plan for hybrids is?"

"Same as the vampires," he said easily. "Obey our laws and keep our existence low-key. The newer generations are tired of the constant war between vampires and shifters. They want to live in peace, be allowed to mate other species, not fear for their children. They've even asked me to help them integrate into society like the shifters are doing."

"Be allowed to mate another species? Have other vampires found their true mate outside of the vampire race?"

"I've learned some interesting things since Sigma went down, Alex. For instance, this war between our species and how it's escalated in the last several decades."

She nodded, interested to hear more. They had all assumed it was technology and its capability to permeate more destruction.

"What if, like you and I sitting here *collaborating*," he gave the word air quotes, "our councils had their own way of working together? I was sent to the equivalent of vampire boarding school, being a royal and all." She had heard he came from a powerful family and was destined to sit on their own council, which explains why vampires were so willing to follow him as he took over. "Some of my fellow classmates and I would hit the town on the weekends, rip it up. But we started hearing talk. So we hit more towns, partied it up everywhere we could, kept our ears open. We started to see patterns in the tragedies that befell our people. Started noticing how vampires who took a heavy interest in a person outside their species often met a horrible fate, along with the human or shifter who had captured their interest."

Alex took a swig of her water. She knew her parents weren't crazy to live in hiding, but they had never shared with her exactly why, other than that they feared each other's council.

"The two deaths were never connected, right? Vampires live in hiding and are rarely involved with another species. Unless we're killing them, drinking from them, or fucking them," he amended. "So my team and I looked into it further. Any humans met with an accident, any shifters killed by vampires, and the vampires who showed too much interest in them were killed by shifters."

So...shifters took care of problem vampires and vice versa. "Nice and tidy."

"Exactly," Demetrius agreed. "The Vampire Council kept the Sigma networks in place to keep hunting shifters. Of course, they wouldn't hesitate to dominate and enslave them, but until then, shifters had their uses."

"And Madame G, and all the chaos she caused, was a handy distraction so they let her go without leashing her in."

"She was such a maniacal bitch." He shook his head grimly. "I'm still finding disturbing evidence of the dark arts she was involved in. Good job on the kill by the way. Love how you rubbed in your heritage at the last minute. Gave it enough time to register, then finished her off." He slid off his stool and went to the fridge to snag a beer. Holding it up to offer her one, she shook her head. He sat back down next to her and took a big swig. "I got stationed in Freemont's Sigma chapter and used it as a front to keep researching our theory."

"The two councils were working together to exterminate trans-species mating?"

"Yep. Another issue I aim to rectify is that shifters have Guardians and, except for a few corrupt exceptions, they protect packs, human mates and all. Vampires have no such protection."

"The Lycan Council's been getting greedy lately and targeting more human mates." Alex couldn't imagine how the two species' governments could work together in any capacity and get away with it.

"I'd imagine two of the West Creek Guardians mating humans didn't sit well. It's one thing when it's the lower ranks, but not the warriors."

Jace wasn't a born Guardian, but he was an excellent one and Cassie was human. Their mating was followed shortly by Mercury and Dani. Obviously, Mercury's DNA was special, so a human having his babies must have been like salt on the human-mating wound.

"I need to prove it, or they'll never leave me and Rhys alone."

"Love, I've been trying to prove it for years. I can't manage to find anyone alive to act as witness."

"They kill every one they target, then?"

"Not necessarily. They may leave the more powerful mates alone, hoping they'll take a new mate and not question the death too much. When my vampires took down the other Sigma chapters, we found prisoners who had been slaughtered as soon as they heard we were coming. Made me wonder what they knew."

Shifters kept prisoners. Each Guardian pack had their own jail and a small prison was at the council's headquarters. Alex wondered what she might find there.

She peeked over at the unconscious Scurn to make sure he was still out cold. "I'll run all this by Bennett. We'll keep you informed if we find anything."

"Ah, yes. Commander Young. I haven't had the pleasure of dealing with him yet. He's not as interested in trying to beat the shit out of me as the previous commander was."

Alex wanted to smirk at the thought of Rhys getting more than a few punches in on Demetrius, but her heart twisted at the reason why. Bennett was wrong. She had hurt Rhys. He was a rock, her rock, but she had given him a few chips.

While her mind threatened to go all melancholy, Demetrius leaned in close. She could feel his breath on her neck.

"Tell me, love, you've gone without for a while?" He rasped into her ear, tickling the short hair that stuck out behind it.

"Demetrius, if one of your fangs so much as touches me, I'm going to pull them both out with my bare hands while I use my foot on your balls for leverage."

He threw his head back and laughed deeply. "My word, Alex," he wheezed between busting his

gut, "I'm glad that shifter hasn't made you weak."
Still chuckling and shaking his head, he finished his
beer. "Ah, I wasn't looking to end my dry streak
anyway."

It wasn't often the male surprised Alex, but
Demetrius retaining some semblance of abstinence
did it. "You goin' soft on me, Big D?"

He grimaced. "Lovely choice of words." He
turned to look at her, his pale greens solemn. "You
know why I liked sex with you even though it was
an ego-crushing event?"

"Ego crushing?"

"Please, love. It hits a male hard when his
partner disappears inside her mind as he's going at
her."

Yeah, she never hid that. It's not like she cared
what he thought, she just needed the sex to serve its
purpose. "Then why?"

"Because it meant something. It was for a
reason. I got your rich blood, you got some intel.
All the club fucking…sure, at first it's a good time.
Then, it's just empty. Feels like an itch that never
gets satisfied, no matter how many screaming cunts
rub on it."

"Nice, D. Nice."

He gave her a shit-eating grin. "Like that, did
ya? I don't always use that word, but when I do, it's
to a beautiful woman."

She rolled her eyes and he laughed again.

"I think I like our new relationship, Alex. This
whole friends with no benefits thing."

Smiling, she tipped her water bottle to his beer for a quick "cheers" and stood up. Time to go. She had to sneak into Bennett's cabin, after knocking loudly so she didn't catch him and Sarah at it *again* and pass along all the information she got tonight.

Pointing to the big vampire guard still passed out in the entryway, she said, "He should wake up shortly. Doc said it'd knock him down for a couple of hours."

"I'll drag him back out to the hallway and let him piss himself thinking he fell asleep on the job." Demetrius grinned wickedly. "It'll be fun to mess with him."

"Nice chatting with you, D. I'll go out the way I came."

"Which is? I'd like to know so I can tighten up security."

She waved him off. "Your security's not bad. But you'll need to reactivate the alarm by the west windows. And your interior cameras aren't three-sixty. Just sayin'. On the difficulty scale of B and E, I'd give it an eight."

"Noted."

Chapter Twelve

The beefy fist nailed him in the gut again. Rhys doubled over, or at least tried to, being tied up as usual.

Mastiff stepped back. "Has she contacted you yet?"

"Yeah, we have mind sex every night."

Another blow to the gut. Rhys coughed, his jaw stretched wide in pain. Months of the same old, same old didn't make it any better. Mastiff hated him more and got a little more brutal every time. Sometimes it took Rhys days to grow teeth back and keep food down before his body healed properly.

It was worth it.

They would be even more ruthless to Alex if they got a hold of her. They might not start out as brutal, but her mouth would get them there. He felt powerless not to be able to help her and the issues she had to go work through on her own. He could do this. He could absorb their anger toward her.

As Rhys' gut throbbed, a soothing wave flowed through his mind. His brows furrowed, his eyes strained to refocus. Letting his senses flare out, he got…nothing. Something? Wait. It seemed like nothing, but something was there, making his inner wolf rise and take note.

Whatever it was didn't feel threatening. Rhys forced himself to look at Mastiff's ugly face sneering at him. If he scanned around the room, Mastiff might get suspicious. Was there anything to get suspicious about? His gut told him yes, but he had no fucking clue why.

"Reach out to her." The Guardian pawn of the council growled, raising his fist in a threat.

"All right, let me try." Rhys closed his eyes and tipped his head back. "Okay. She says fuck you." Rhys opened his eyes so the body part that got nailed next wasn't a surprise.

Mastiff's sneer coiled his lips as he pulled back for more force. Before his anvil fist could reach Rhys' face, it was jerked back and twisted. Mastiff's body angled with it, thanks to the strong feminine hand on his shoulder. Using the momentum of the male, Rhys watched as Alex pushed him head first into the wall. Not waiting for the rebound, she booted him in the kidneys.

Rhys was shocked to see her, but not at all surprised that she was able to get in unnoticed. He wrenched at his chains. He'd been in them often enough, and long enough, to get a good feel for them. Not only were they solid, they were lined with silver. But damn, if he needed to sacrifice a hand to help Alex, he would.

Before Mastiff could recover from being thrown into the wall and then kicked, Alex withdrew a dart gun and shot a tiny red arrow into the goliath's flank. With a snarl, Mastiff spun, lashing an arm out that Alex deflected and danced away from. The male gritted his teeth together and charged at her, his fists ready to fly.

Rhys' rage launched him at the guard, chair and all. With a yell, he took to his feet and barreled into the male right before he reached Alex. Mastiff stumbled to the side, while Rhys kept toppling until he hit the floor. The force of the hit turned him enough that he fell onto his side. After he landed, Rhys used his feet to spin and kick a leg out to trip Mastiff when he made another lunge for Alex.

Alex had another dart ready. When Mastiff hit the floor, she pumped the red dart into his back. He struggled to get up and she booted him in the head.

"Just to be sure," she said, as Rhys heard the male's body thud limply onto the floor.

Rhys let her rich voice roll through him, relaxing him in all the right places, tightening him in even better ones. The throbbing agony in his gut was a distant memory with her in the room.

He couldn't see her from the position he was now laying in. But what he did see before he fell was that she looked like Agent X—dressed in tight black leather and armed to her pearly whites with blades and guns.

"Sweet Mother Earth it's good to see you." Rhys was glad he could say that. If Alex hadn't gotten there when she did, his mouth would have been shredded.

"I noticed you were a little tied up."

He heard her move over Mastiff, confirming he was really out. Then her footsteps moved next to him. She yanked him upright with the back and seat of the metal chair and set all four legs on the floor.

"Damn, he must keep the keys outside the room. I'll have to get your chains off the fun way." She squatted down to pick the lock on the chain around his torso that secured him to the back of the chair. He used the moment to look her over.

She looked fine. Damn fine. Her eyes were still their normal brilliant green, but a calmness had settled into them that he hadn't noticed before. Her new hairstyle was edgy, but ultra-feminine, just like she was.

"How did you flash in here?" Vamps couldn't flash somewhere they'd never been before. Rhys was outraged thinking she had been in the interrogation room before.

Those vibrant green eyes rose to meet his as she finished her work on the first lock. "Malcolm gave me your beating schedule after he supplied a detailed outline of the council's facilities. I made sure to step in here and peak around before you arrived."

Alex moved behind him to work on the cuffs around his wrists. The heat of her fingers and just having her close was screwing with his senses.

"How do you keep your scent tapered down like that?" His mind and body knew she was close by and his mating instincts flared, but he wanted to be enveloped in her scent. It dulled the agony of his time spent with Mastiff.

"It's a trick Sigma taught us. It's like using my hypnosis to amplify the other scents around us, so ours becomes camouflaged. Mentally taxing, but effective."

He felt tugs on his wrists as she worked on the lock. "Can you teach my pack that?" Then Rhys remembered he was no longer in charge. "I mean, Bennett might think it's a good idea."

She leaned up to speak softly into his ear, causing heat to spiral down to his groin. "Don't worry, Rhys. Bennett hasn't warmed up to the commander position at all."

He turned his head toward her, his lips inches from hers. The cuffs dropped away. He didn't waste any time snaking an arm around her waist, drawing her up and across his lap. Draping one leg over, Alex straddled his lap and rested arms over his shoulders.

Wrapping his arms around her waist, he leaned into her neck to breathe in her subtle wildflower scent. "The council won't reinstate me."

Idly running her fingers in patterns on the back of his head, she unconsciously rocked her hips into him. "They won't have a say if they're not around anymore."

Rhys jerked his head back. "The council, or the males on it?"

Alex shrugged casually. "Both. Either. Whatever works."

Narrowing his eyes on her, he tightened his hold and rocked his own hips up into her, seeking a margin of relief from the strain behind his zipper. "What does my beautiful mate have planned?"

A small smile touched her lips at his compliment. "Getting you out of here. Then searching their secret prison."

Rhys frowned as he thought it over. "Wouldn't it have been better to leave me here while you searched the prison? Then my absence, or the attack on Mastiff, wouldn't set off any alarms."

She drew her lips back slightly, baring a tiny amount of fang. The view went straight to his manhood, because his last memory of seeing her fangs was when she ran one down his length. Most. Erotic. Experience. Ever.

She leaned down to nip his bottom lip. "Did you leave me hanging at Sigma?"

Rhys groaned and pulled her closer. "Mastiff's a big pussy cat. I'da been all right."

Alex chuckled, running her tongue along his lower lip to catch the drop of blood she drew. Rhys could no longer take it. He captured her mouth with his own. Surprising even himself, he didn't go further. His lips on her lips. Contact with his mate. It was what his body craved after six months, any sort of contact. Being deprived of her dreams had been the toughest part of his confinement, of her being gone.

He broke off the kiss. "Are you here to stay?"

Her lips were a breadth away. "Maybe. I can't live openly under the Lycan Council as it stands. Whether we replace the council, or come up with another form of government all together, it would depend on if it's…adequate."

He swiped his lips across hers again. "If they seek to control you again?"

"Exactly." This time, she caught his mouth and coaxed his lips open.

Rhys responded greedily, wanting to taste his mate, be as close to her as their situation would allow. Their tongues intertwined, their hands roaming each other's body.

Alex was the first to break contact, her breathing ragged. "As much as I want to continue this, we need to move while the big guy is down."

Alex was completely right. They had limited time and an unconscious body in the room. It wasn't like he was trying to argue, but his body was on fire for her.

"You hit him twice," Rhys pointed out.

"He's a big dude."

"If you got the tranqs from Doc, he'll be down for a while. Doc knows what he's doing."

A smile tipped the corner of Alex's mouth. "I like that old shifter."

Rhys nipped at her lip again. "I think he's younger than me."

She looked surprised. "Really? You look so damn hot, all virile and shit, I forget you're a few centuries old."

He let a stupid grin spread across his face.

Giving him a saucy grin in return, she stood up and stepped back. He followed, so they were just as close standing as they had been sitting.

"Are we going to try to get into the prison?" He was healing from his beating already and ready to act physically instead of dream walking.

Rhys had never been able to break through whatever barrier the council had setup around their main prison. Except for making it into Mastiff's dreams and coercing the male to show him memories of prisoners, Rhys almost would've thought there really was no prison.

Almost.

The mental void in the basement of the council's facilities was a pretty clear indication that there was something down there that the council didn't want others to get to.

"I met with Demetrius," Alex paused as a disgruntled expression crossed Rhys' face. "Nothing happened."

"I know. I just don't like him."

She didn't bother hiding her smirk. "I think the feeling's mutual. At least you two can be big boys and work together. Anyhoodles, he said when they overthrew the other Sigma chapters around the country, some prisoners died mysteriously. Like, the vampires running Sigma didn't want them to spill any secrets about why they were imprisoned. He thinks the councils have had an 'I'll bite your jugular and let you bite mine' agreement, and that maybe the shifters are holding their own people."

"That would explain how they found out about you." Rhys couldn't believe it. The councils were working together? It was hard enough for the Lycan Council to work with its own people.

"To take care of those pesky trans-species mates."

Understanding dawned on him. Of course. It would appear like any other vampire-shifter hate killing, not a targeted attack. "Who would be imprisoned then?"

"We're hoping shifters who either found out the council ordered a hit on their loved one, or are refusing to give up information on where their human or vampire mate is."

With that kind of witness, bringing down the council might actually be possible. His dream surveillance could only go so far. A witness to backup what Rhys saw would seal the deal against the council. "I walked in Mastiff's dreams. I got him to start dreaming about his job. He was torturing a female of our kind. Kept asking where her mate was."

"Maybe she's still down there."

Rhys shook his head grimly. "The dream cut off after—" Rhys grimaced at the memory of what he saw. "I don't think he meant to push her too far, but I got the impression she didn't survive that round."

Alex looked behind her at the prone form of Mastiff. "Should I kill him?"

"No," Rhys said adamantly. "I don't want to give the council any more reason to come after you. Mastiff's not that bright. He's the brawn behind the brain. He'll get dealt with when we go against who's behind all this."

"Let's chain him up. He can mentally call anyone he wants, but," she grinned wickedly, "I can fix the lock to this room so it'll be hard for anyone to get to him."

Alex took the male's feet while Rhys worked on his hands. After the male's hands were secured, Rhys straightened, eyeing the huge body on the floor. "Do you have any more darts?"

"Why Rhys," Alex purred, causing his body to tighten even more, "need you ask?" She withdrew the dart gun, already loaded with two more darts and pumped them both into Mastiff. Rhys couldn't help the pull of a grin at his lips. Yeah, all that tranq could kill the male and Alex damn well knew it.

She looked at him like *what?* and shoved the gun back into its holster. "Let's jet."

Rhys had no other option but to follow her, she had the layout of the building. Watching the sway of her hips in those leathers, he didn't mind at all.

***

Alex trotted cautiously into the hallway and led her mate into a side storage room where she had stashed his gear. She felt all girly to his face lighting up when he saw his stuff.

His intense hazel eyes warmed toward her. "Thank you."

"Bennett wanted to make sure you got it back." She didn't know why she didn't want to take credit for doing something nice and thinking about her mate. Maybe it felt too intimate, like she cared. Of course Rhys knew she cared. Maybe it was because she didn't want to disappoint him even more if she had to take off again.

Rhys ignored the comment, and the reasons behind it, and stripped his prison shirt and pants off without shame. Alex didn't bother looking away. The male was glorious in his nudity. Hard, sculpted muscles and—drool ran down her fangs—those little striations along the ribs that acted like a marquis for rippled abs. The muscles around his hip bones, running south, flattened as they reached the jutting member standing proudly between his legs.

It's not like she hadn't seen him before, she'd just never seen him completely nude before, where she could really get a good look. So, damn, why did it have to be there? Why did it have to be now, when she didn't know if she had to leave him again?

"See something that interests you?" he growled low. His hooded eyes watched her reaction as he stepped into his pants.

She cocked an eyebrow and decided not to say anything. Crossing her arms and reclining back against the wall, she took in the reverse strip show he was putting on.

Covering up that body seemed like crime. As his bare skin disappeared under his tactical clothing, she was rewarded with watching him smoothly and capably go through his weapons. He systematically checked knives and guns, and holstered them all over his body. Gawd, the male was a stud.

She knew enough not be insulted that he felt like he had to double-check his gear. It was what smart warriors did. She'd have done the same and she had, many times, when E would pop in with her stuff after a bad punishment session.

Once Rhys was done, he gave her an expectant look, as if waiting for her to lead the way. She had the entire facility committed to memory. It was like a campus, and the building they were in was where the council conducted all their business. Hence, it was where they kept the prisoners. The less a prisoner had to be moved for a tribunal, the better.

She wasn't going to lead him anywhere. Instead, she grabbed his arm and flashed him to the closet she had remained hidden in while waiting for the guard to transport Rhys.

Suddenly reappearing in the dark, Rhys swayed next to her, trying to adjust after the flash.

"That's a handy way to avoid security cameras," he muttered, giving his head one last good shake.

"It's awesome. I can name a ton of times flashing would've gotten my ass out of pickle. If Mastiff can remain unconscious and dream of large women, we should have two solid hours. We need to get into the interior prison, find a witness, and get as far away from here as possible."

"We'll need to free everyone."

He had to be joking, but Rhys didn't do shit like that. "Depending on the shape they're in, we'd be lucky to escape with even one witness," she countered. If there's even a witness to the council's ill deeds to be found.

"Alex," Rhys spoke evenly, his tone leaving no room for argument, "I realize how you had to do things in the past. You had to draw the line for self-preservation. I can't do that. My duty, my *nature*, is to protect my species. I can't leave innocent prisoners behind to face the fear and wrath of the council."

Rhys' words sunk in. When she was with Sigma and trying to stay alive so she could kill Madame G, her decisions had often been the lesser of two evils. He was right. If they got into the prison, discovered innocent occupants, it would be on her conscience if they met with a bitter end. Once the council discovered Rhys was missing, their prison broken into—and then out of—they might terminate those left behind in order to keep their secret.

"Fine," she sighed. In the dark of the storage closet, her keen eyes picked up the amusement in his. "Malcolm only knew there was a prison, but he'd never been in it. He and Harrison tried to get in there, not realizing how protected it was. Another try and the old bastards would've gotten too suspicious."

"He gave you a detailed layout of everything around the prison, though?"

"At least we have that. I've found a weak point where we can make our entry." She hesitated.

"Is there a catch?"

"Depends if you like tight places." The words left Alex's mouth before she caught her unintentional innuendo. Not that it would've changed what she had said. Heat flared in his gaze and his lust spiked a notch. Since there was no time to act on any of their desires, she continued. "Ductwork."

"Seriously?" He sounded even less thrilled than she felt.

"Cameras and highly specified access are on every entrance. The combo of the two makes it too difficult in the time we have. There's a ton of ductwork and it's sizable, so I think we can get through it."

"Where do we enter?"

Alex pointed up to the grate lodged high in the wall. She had already removed the front panel, so all they needed to do was crawl up inside.

"Beauty before age," she said sweetly, and leaped up.

***

The only benefit of crawling through narrow ducts behind his mate should've been getting to watch her ass slither ahead of him. But with the lack of light, and their bodies incased in black, not even that show was on display. All he could do was scoot along and keep his gear from scraping on the surface and making noise.

After at least fifteen uncomfortable minutes, she finally came to a stop.

We're at the main grate into the cellblock. I'll remove the cover and identify any surveillance.

Even his ears could barely pick up her work on the grate. Less than a minute later, the cover was off, and she was searching their surroundings.

I can see only two cameras. This grate lies at the end of a dual row of cells.

How many?

Five on each side, less than half filled.

Rhys could only scent shifters through the opening. *Three shifters to rescue. Not bad.*

If they can walk. Let me go in first. I can disable the cameras. Doubt they get watched that closely.

Alex rolled out of the grate and hung down out of the opening, not jumping to the floor. When Rhys scooted forward so he could look out, he saw why. She was swinging her body to gain enough momentum to reach the camera angled to view the cells on his right. He watched as she swung up, twisted in the air, and tapped a button on the side. As she started to fall, she flashed.

He looked across the row of small, narrow cells lining each side of the room to the camera kitty-corner on the far wall. Completely impressed with his mate's skill, he watched her reappear in the air right next to the far camera and tap another button before falling the rest of the way to the floor. She landed in a silent crouch and peered up at him.

I couldn't do any more than shut them off, so we might not have much time.

Rhys rolled out and landed lightly on his feet. The shifters in the cells eased toward the bars. They had scented Rhys and probably caught Alex's movement.

"Let's make it quick," Alex said in a low voice. "Who are you, and why are you here?"

On Rhys' right, a dark-haired female peered out of the bars in her cell. Straight across from her in consecutive cells, were two male shifters—one who appeared older than Rhys and one younger. Rhys' anger spiked. The only reason the males were in the cells directly across from the female was probably to violate her privacy. There was nothing she could do that would remain hidden from the two across from her.

"I'm Sylva." The female's voice was shaky. Rhys recognized her from Mastiff's dreams. She had been under the male's fists more than once.

"Don't answer them," the older male cut in. "We don't know who they are or what they want."

"We can help you." Rhys stepped forward so they could inspect him.

"Guardian." The sneer on the younger male's face told Rhys a lot.

"Chill dude." Alex moved forward also. "This male pissed the council off, so he's on Guardian hiatus. Now answer me." Her voice left no room for argument.

But argue, the young male did. "Or what?"

Alex's ice-cold green eyes landed on the young male, causing him to shrink back.

"I-I killed my mate." The young female stammered, afraid for the male arguing with Alex.

"Sylva!" The younger male looked frantic for Sylva.

"Did he deserve it?" Alex's bluntness and the shifter's shock at her question made Rhys' lips almost twitch into a smile.

Sylva's eyes fell to the floor. "No, of course not."

"That sounded like what the council wants to hear. I'm guessing he did deserve it."

Sylva nodded, her limp black hair swinging slightly with the motion, and she finally raised her gaze to meet Alex's. "He coerced me into a mating ceremony by bribing my father. I could've forgiven him for that, but not for the way he treated me."

It was a story Rhys had heard time and again during his years as a Guardian. Older unmated shifter afraid of going feral forces a mating. It rarely ended well, for either mate.

Alex and Rhys turned their attention to the males. They were in separate cells, but it was easy to see that the two males were related.

"Clock's ticking boys." Alex's foot tapped, her fingers were hooked over her tactical belt.

The older male spoke first. He tipped his head toward the cell next to him. "This is my son, Damon. I'm William."

"I won't be calling you anything as I get the fuck out of here because you two are taking too long." Alex paused to assess the mutinous look on Damon's face.

Rhys decided to prod things along. By his furtive glances, William was waiting on his son, but Damon didn't plan on saying a word.

"Either one of you have a vampire mate who suddenly got killed or disappeared?"

Damon's head snapped up. "How did you—" He realized he was going to confess something and snapped his mouth shut.

"We are being detained until we tell the council where Damon's girlfriend is," William filled in.

"So she's still alive?"

Damon's jaw clenched.

William wrapped his hands around the bars. "Damon was on the phone with Lily when he heard her getting attacked. He rushed over there, calling me on the way. I was the only one that knew about them."

"I thought Dad turned me in." The tone of his voice sounded like he regretted doubting his father's innocence.

"Damon has plenty of friends who could've noticed he kept running off to see a female he never brought around them. It would've been easy for them to smell vampire on him."

"This Lily was attacked, but she's still alive?" Alex's sharp eyes pinned Damon again.

Damon got a faraway look in his eyes. "I think so. She was bleeding so much. I got there just in time. Two shifters were after her, Guardians, and I distracted them. I almost didn't make it, but Dad showed up."

"We helped her flash away," William clarified. "She wouldn't have made it far, but it was enough that they couldn't sense her. Now we're here."

"Do you know what pack the Guardians were with?" Rhys asked.

"They're here, the council's pack." Damon's look was dark. "The big one who keeps trying to beat me until I lead them to her, and another guy. I haven't had a trial, or a hearing of any kind. No one knows we're here, and we've been here for months."

He exchanged a look with Alex, who bobbed her head slightly. "Listen up, bitches. I'm gonna flash y'all out of here, but I'm starting with Damon. You, my boy, get to be our witness against the council."

William shifted. "So this has happened to others? Wait. You can flash?"

Alex pointed to herself with both thumbs. "Hybrid. We gotta go."

She reached out for Damon's hand, who snatched his back. "I'm not helping you find Lily."

"No, you're going to help me take the fucking council down."

Rhys jumped in with an explanation after realizing the male had been incarcerated for a while and didn't realize what was going on in the world. "The vampires are involved in a civil war. Their people found out what they've been doing. Seems both councils had the same idea when it came to vampire and shifter matings."

"Kill them?" William didn't sound surprised, not after what his son experienced.

"What about me?" The soft voice asked behind them.

"Sylva, would we forget about you?" Alex shot her a dazzling smile. "You'll have to be flashed after these two, though. The witnesses take priority."

Can you flash that many times, with passengers?

Dunno. Looks like we're going to find out. Alex held her hand out at Damon and waggled her fingers.

Damon gave it a dubious look before grabbing on.

"By the way, after we arrive, you'll feel like you just chugged a six-pack and jumped on a rollercoaster."

It wasn't until the two disappeared that Rhys realized he didn't think to ask where she planned on taking them.

Chapter Thirteen

Alex arrived at the safe house where Malcolm and Harrison were waiting. It was a cabin deep in the woods that could be used for boat fishing in the summer and ice fishing in the winter.

She still held Damon's hand. She had to or he'd have spiraled into the wall. When he doubled over, she finally let go so he could prop himself up on his knees as he tried to regain his equilibrium.

"We're here, ladies," she called, knowing the twins were somewhere nearby. They kept this room unoccupied for the sole purpose of her flashing into it.

Harrison bust through the door, scowling. He was armed and his gun was raised, but he lowered it after he assessed the situation.

Malcolm, identical to Harrison with his shaggy chestnut-brown hair and golden eyes, came striding in behind him. "You're so obnoxious, Alex."

His grin made her grin back. Harrison kept scowling. She liked the twins. Her history with them wasn't as peppered with altercations as the rest of the Guardians in Rhys' pack.

"You two are my boys, you know that?"

Malcolm's dimple had to be the reason why so many females threw themselves at him. He couldn't hold a candle to Rhys in her opinion, but she could see his appeal.

"You say that to all the twin Guardians you come across."

"So far, I have." She looked down to where Damon was bent over, hands on his knees, heaving. "This is our primary witness. There's one more and another prisoner, then Rhys."

She flashed back to the prison. Rhys stood in the same spot and Sylva's violet eyes were wide with what she was seeing.

"Good?" Alex asked Rhys.

"So far, but I think they're coming."

She held out her hand to William, who didn't hesitate to grab onto it.

Flashing back to the cabin, she went through the same process with him. She strongly suspected he would've hurled if he'd eaten anything in the last few hours.

Malcolm was pacifying an apprehensive Damon, so she caught Harrison's eye. "This is witness number two, Damon's dad."

The male nodded, ever the somber twin. Alex suspected he had deep-seated issues of some sort. *Don't we all.*

Fatigue had begun settling in, she took a deep breath and flashed. Back in the prison, she jumped to the side, damn near getting rammed into by Rhys entangled with a guard.

Shit, they'd been discovered. Another large shifter was fighting to get into the room but an unconscious Guardian blocked the door. Rhys had been busy while she was gone.

Take Sylva to wherever you go, then flash back into the closet, Rhys grunted into her mind.

Alex spun to hold her hand out to Sylva, only to find the female cowering back in her cell, gazing on in fear at the Guardian who Rhys was busy with. How the hell did the timid little female kill her mate?

Letting out a frustrated breath, Alex flashed into the cell and grabbed Sylva. The girl squeaked, barely able to finish the sound before they appeared at the cabin.

The young female dropped to her knees and Alex almost joined her. Her heart was racing, like she'd run all day and eaten nothing. Could she even get back to Rhys?

Alex didn't have time to waste, but she needed a few seconds before she flashed again. She looked at Sylva.

"You didn't kill him did you? You're covering for someone."

Sylva's eyes widened, but Alex didn't miss the steel that lined her gaze. Ah, she was covering for someone who *helped* her kill her mate.

"No big," Alex reassured her. "There's two Guardians here to protect you. Don't let them scare you. They're complete dicks, but straight-up honorable."

Confusion defined Sylva's frown with Alex's statement, until Harrison came into the room, then alarm crossed her features. Alex didn't have time to reassure her anymore.

"I'm going to get Rhys," she announced as she rose to stand. The slight sway when she fully straightened wasn't unexpected.

Harrison's gaze narrowed on her. "Are you okay?"

The male usually let his brother do the talking. It wasn't in Alex's favor that she looked like shit enough for him to inquire about her.

"Totes." Alex flashed to the closet, feeling more than a little lethargic. Like she could eat a big steak, with a pound of bacon chaser, and sleep all night.

Her vision was swimming, so she took a deep breath. Only then did she hear metallic thumping. She furrowed her brows and listened closer. Then it dawned on her. She and Rhys had been so quiet going through the ductwork, but the sounds she was hearing now was that of a large body thunking around in it.

Or more than one large body.

She jumped up and pulled herself into the duct. *Rhys, are you trying to get back to the closet?*

Yes. Even mentally, he sounded out of breath. They must be trying to follow him.

I'll make my way toward you. All we need to do is grab hands.

'Kay.

She heard more thumps and grunts. Whoever was behind Rhys was getting Rhys' boot plastered all over his face.

Army-crawling her way through the duct, sweat trickled down her brow. Maybe it was the enclosed space. Or maybe it was because she never flashed so many times in a row, so quickly, as she had the last few minutes. Hopefully it was a space issue. She still had a two-hundred and fifty pound male to flash away.

Alex was moving faster than Rhys. They were almost within touching distance.

Grab my hand. She reached one arm out as far as she could, they were only feet away from each other.

Don't flash until I tell you. The fucker keeps grabbing my legs to drag me backward.

His strong hand enveloped her forearm. Relief poured through her. She closed her eyes and concentrated on the cabin, waiting for Rhys' signal.

He jerked as he kicked his leg back to shake the shifter off. Scooting back, Alex tried to give Rhys more room to move ahead so he wasn't so easy to grab again.

"Mother. Fucker." Rhys gritted out the words before a mighty clang shook the whole duct. It was

followed by another, then another, as Rhys
repeatedly slammed his boot back.

Now!

Immediately, her senses were flooded with
fresh air. What the…

Opening her eyes, she saw patches of dirt with
new green life poking through. Son of a bitch.

Rhys still held onto her arm, but groaned and
rolled over on his back. "Is this the meeting spot?"

She rolled to her back also. Above her were
branches with budding leaves and blue sky. "Sure
isn't."

He surprised her by chuckling. "Glad I was
your last passenger, then."

She smiled and they both lay in silence. It was
nice. Peaceful. Alex had many peaceful experiences
in the past six months, but it was better with Rhys.

It would sure be nice to stay with him.

"Any idea where we're at?"

"Maybe somewhere between the council's
headquarters and the family lake cabin the twins
were meeting us at. I'd say a forty-mile difference
and we're… in the middle?"

"I know where the cabin's at." Rhys finally
released her arm to sit up. "Malcolm told me about
it when they first joined my pack."

Alex followed suit, sitting up. She let her
senses roam. They were in the wilderness. Vast
wilderness. West Creek and Freemont were
surrounded by woods, but were still large
metropolitan areas. The two cities were ideal for

shifters because they could take a short day trip and run in the woods, then return and blend in with humans.

The council's headquarters was farther north, where there were more trees than buildings in any given town. Lakes dotted the countryside, and only a few highways connected the small logging and fishing towns.

"I guess we start walking." Alex jumped up and stretched, only to feel the burn of Rhys' gaze upon her.

He stood slowly, moving like a predator, and her heart rate increased a notch. "I remember the last time we were alone in the woods."

She passed him a seductive smile. "Do you want me to reenact that scene again?"

He glided close to her, his gaze intense. "Oh yes, but not now." Rhys lifted his hand to her mouth, his thumb stroking her lower lip. "The next time I'm in you, it won't be here, but," he trailed his hand down her neck, stroking her breasts on his way down, where he cupped her sex, "here."

Oh yeah, she wanted that, too.

"First," he wrapped the same arm around her waist, "we need to get to a town and figure out where we're at."

"I could try to flash again."

He brought his other arm around her so she was in his embrace. "Not until you rest up, get some sleep."

"Sleep?" Her tone was coy.

A slow smile spread across the lips she couldn't quit staring at. "Sleep. After we get...reacquainted, you need sleep."

***

Rhys had never been in such a hurry to get somewhere so quickly. He and Alex ran through the trees, the terrain not as rugged as he was used to around West Creek. Both of them sensed civilization nearby and ran toward it, twice having to circle around good-sized lakes. The trip would've been much faster as wolves, but they had nothing to carry their clothing and gear in. On two legs, the trip was enjoyable, even though hunger gnawed at him. Alex looked worn, but it didn't slow her stride at all. After months of confinement, even with the recovering he'd had to do after his sessions with Mastiff, the run invigorated him.

Daylight was fading and that would probably work in their favor. They wouldn't be as easily identifiable to anyone in town if the council sent out their descriptions to nearby packs.

"Three miles," Alex huffed ahead of him.

They took turns taking the lead because there were too many obstacles to run side by side. Rhys liked when she ran ahead of him; she really was something to watch. Her strong, lithe body maneuvering over rocks and around tree limbs, climbing the steeper inclines without any hitch in her stride, she was made for the woods. She was made for him.

He just had to figure out how to keep her.

From the beginning, it seemed like their relationship was doomed. Sigma had been decimated, thanks to that bastard Demetrius. Alex should be free, but because of her blood, she was now hunted. He let her go six months ago, sensed she needed time, but now she was back and he wanted to make sure she didn't leave his side again. Whatever it took.

Easier said than done. They were at the cusp of rebellion, moving their pawns into place to topple their own government. Could it be as simple as replacing a few leaders on the council?

Nothing was ever simple.

Cresting a rise, Rhys picked up clear scents of civilization. Then he could see buildings and hear the dull drones of vehicles in the distance.

Alex pulled up short. "Do you see what I see?"

Rhys squinted into the darkness and scanned the expanse where the trees were thinning and small homes dotted the landscape. A sign with half the neon burned out barely stood above the rooftops.

"Motel."

Alex grinned and wiped her face. They were both covered in grit and sweat. "Perfect. It looks like one of those strip motels with the entrances on the outside."

"We can bust into one of the rooms and hope they don't realize it's occupied until we're gone."

Alex's lush lips stretched even further, and her eyes twinkled. "Or, I could pay for it and hypno the clerk into thinking I'm an old blond lady passing through."

Rhys blinked. He had guns, knives, and enough silver lined his blades to pay for a whole stretch of rooms. But no money, in any form. "You have enough cash?"

"Please. I didn't reach the ripe old age of thirty by being unprepared." She took off again.

He had no choice but to follow, and he did so gladly. Watching that fine ass sway in front of him was a sight he'd never tire of.

As the buildings became more frequent and closer together, they both slowed their pace. It was completely dark now, but they still utilized as much cover as possible.

The Treetop Motel sat on the edge of town, where Main Street turned into a highway to nowhere. The building was nestled into a copse of trees that at one time may have been a beautiful shade. Now, the trees were scraggly and nearing the end of their lifespan. Every windstorm, the owner probably prayed one of them didn't topple over and crush the roof.

They made their way to the edge of the clearing around the motel. Alex unbuckled her shoulder holster and tactical belt. When each one slipped off, she handed it to Rhys. After her most obvious weapons were removed, she ran a hand through her hair to shake out any debris and ruffled it until it hung over her eyes. She untucked her shirt and tied the bottom until a tantalizing strip of belly was visible.

"It's easier to sway their mind when they're distracted."

Rhys pulled his gaze up to hers. "What if it's a woman?"

Alex winked at him. "Chicks look too. Be right back." She jogged around the motel to the entrance.

Rhys let his senses roam. Whatever town this was, it seemed mostly human. That would benefit them greatly. There wasn't much activity to be heard, other than some revving motors that told him the younger crowd was out and about for the night. He counted only three cars that used the road running past the motel in the time Alex was gone.

When she came jogging back, she was holding some papers in her hand.

"Everything go okay?" He didn't doubt her, but couldn't help asking.

"The sixteen-year-old clerk didn't stand a chance. Those young minds are like Play-Doh. We are Mr. and Mrs. Johnson, on our way to a family reunion." She waved the papers in her hand. "I also grabbed a map and a brochure of everything to do in this great city, population twenty-five hundred."

Sweet. Now they knew where they were and could figure out how far away they were from the twin's cabin.

"Lead the way, Mrs. Johnson."

The motel had real keys, not digital cards. Alex let them into a sparse room that held a queen-size bed with a threadbare maroon comforter, a tiny flat-screen TV, and worn wooden tables. It smelled stale, but clean.

"The kid said there was still one place open that delivers pizza, but we'd better call now because it closes soon."

Rhys' stomach growled in agreement. He found the postcard for the pizza place next to the phone and dialed in their order.

Alex headed to the bathroom. "I'm going to clean-up so I can be done by the time I have to convince the pizza guy I'm matronly Mrs. Johnson."

***

Alex let the spray hit her in the face, wash over the caked-on dirt and cemented-in perspiration. Several hours running in fresh air and untouched woods with her mate was glorious. Who could ask for more?

Any memories she could make with Rhys would be cherished. The council wouldn't leave her alone. Even if she and Rhys could prove their case against them and how they hunted mates, it was a stretch to believe she would ever be truly free. There was no way Rhys could leave his pack and run with her. He was a Guardian, through and through, and his people would need him now more than ever.

She shut off the water and grabbed a thin towel from the rack. The Treetop Motel wasn't the Hilton, but she'd stayed in worse. Once she was mostly dry, she threw on only her shirt, and wrapped the towel around her waist. She picked up the rest of her clothes from the bathroom floor and strode out of the small bathroom. Rhys sat on the bed with the map spread out. He glanced up at her, his eyes flaring with appreciation as he took in the way her shirt clung to her torso. His gaze slowly wandered down to where the towel ended and her bare legs started.

"We're not far from the lake cabin," he said, his voice rough.

"Good. Then I can convince our friendly pizza deliverer to let us use his phone."

The green in his hazel eyes gleamed as they roamed over her legs. Delicious heat pooled in her stomach and traveled further down. She contemplated going to him, considering what would happen next. The knock at the door interrupted the moment.

The pizza smelled delightful, even through the closed door. Alex grabbed cash out of her pants and dropped them, and the rest of her clothing, on the table before answering the door.

Catching the eyes of the young delivery driver, she murmured the same description of herself she gave to the motel clerk. Young minds were like slicing through room-temp butter.

"You're going to let us use your phone and not remember a thing."

The boy, with his eyes glazed over, handed over his cell. Rhys came up behind the door, remaining out of sight to make convincing the teen easier for Alex.

Alex snatched the phone and told the boy to hold still. "Duuude," she muttered, handing the cell over to Rhys, "No wonder the kid's slinging pizza. That cell must've cost a fortune."

"I sure didn't have anything like this at his age." Rhys punched in Malcolm's number.

"The whole wheel thing was still pretty new when you were his age."

Rhys held the phone to his ear, amusement shining in his eyes. "Hey, it's me. We can get to you in the morning. I want Alex to rest before she flashes again. Are the witnesses okay?" He paused while Alex tried to hear Malcolm's response. "Nah. Wait 'til we get there and then we'll figure out how to contact Bennett. His phone won't be secure."

Rhys hit disconnect and returned the phone to her. She went into the call history and deleted everything, then gave it back to the kid. Once he handed over the pizzas, she hit him again with her hypnosis.

She was darn near drooling over the delicious smells coming from the boxes. It wasn't the protein packed meal most shifters preferred, but she'd heard Rhys ask for triple sausage.

They both plopped down on the bed, and devoured the greasy slices and two-liter soda.

"I'm gonna hit the shower." Rhys stood and stripped down while Alex unabashedly watched. With one last promising look at her, he disappeared into the bathroom.

Alex pushed the pizza boxes and empty bottle onto the floor, and kicked them over by the garbage. Pulling out the map, she spread it across the bed and lay on her belly to study it.

She had just pinpointed the area where the cabin was compared to the town they were in, when Rhys opened the bathroom door. Glancing over her shoulder, she saw that he was completely naked, filling the doorway with his considerable mass.

He was waiting for her to make the first move. The towel slipped from her waist as she rolled over and sat up. She stripped off her shirt, dropping it to the floor. The map was pushed off the bed to fall on top of her discarded shirt.

Reclining on one hand, her knees drawn up so she wasn't completely open to him, she beckoned him over.

Hesitating a moment, he finally came to the foot of the bed. The burn in his eyes showed her how much he restrained himself.

"I'm ready." To prove her point, she lay all the way down and held her arms out to him.

Again, he hesitated. While she was fairly sure she wouldn't hit panic mode again, she could see why he was afraid of pushing her past her comfort zone.

She sat up. The position put her face almost level with his straining manhood, yet she tried to keep her eyes above the navel. Tonight was about connecting, being present. Putting her mouth on him would certainly connect them, but she wanted more.

His gaze roamed her body and returned to unite with hers. Clasping his hands, she pulled him over her as she lay back again. He came down over her carefully, not settling his weight on top of her.

Her legs anchored on each side of him, her knees moved up to cradle him. She let go of his hands, splaying her fingers across his hard chest, reveling in the feel of his warm skin and the way the solid wall of muscle expanded with each breath.

Rhys kept his weight on his hands and knees, no part of him touching her. He was being more than cautious.

Reaching up to cup his face, she brought his head down to hers. The closer his body came to lying on top of her, the more she wanted to feel him pressed against her, head to toe. Their lips met in a tender kiss, and he groaned, leaning in. His rigid length rested against her belly, heat radiating between them, but he still held himself off her.

Swiping her tongue over his lips, she coaxed him into deepening their kiss. At the same time he opened to meet her tongue with his, she tightened her knees at his sides to bring him in closer.

Their tongues tangled, tasted, and caressed, each taking their time. She bathed in his scent, reveled in the feel of him, the heat of him, the pressure of him.

At last, he settled fully on top of her, and instead of freezing or stiffening, she rolled her hips up into him. He rocked his in response, his lips tearing away from hers to move down her face and kiss her neck.

He caressed her sides with his hands as she wrapped her arms around his shoulders. His lips seared a path down her neck as he moved one hand between her thighs to her center. She was achingly wet for him, a fact that made him growl as soon as his hand cupped her sex.

Loosening the hold of her knees, she gave him more room. His strong fingers found her swollen nub and rubbed languid circles that might seem relaxed, but was anything but. She wanted the pleasure to go on forever, trying not to urge him to move faster.

His mouth crashed down on hers, his tongue starting a dance that mimicked the thrusting of intercourse. If that wasn't a heady enough experience for her, he adjusted his body so he could use his thumb to circle her clit while he inserted a finger to match the pace of his tongue.

The combination was explosive. She gasped into his mouth and wrapped her legs around him.

The pressure was building, the intensity staggering, and when she thought she was going to fall apart in his arms, he abruptly withdrew his finger and removed his hand.

Her eyes flew open when he broke off the kiss, wondering why he would stop. He was gazing down at her with complete need and adoration.

"I want to see this." The veins in his neck protruded from the effort of holding himself in restraint.

She peered down to him moving his shaft into position at her entrance. Her gaze rose to meet his. Her hips lifted, seeking to be filled with everything Rhys could give her. He could've pushed in, buried himself to the hilt. She wanted him to, but he didn't. His stare anchored hers with the exquisite pressure of his slow invasion. She wanted to use her legs to push him in fully, but it was like they both sensed how monumental this moment was, how long they both had waited to be together.

Rhys pushed in another inch and she couldn't help it, she rolled her hips up, her body trying to grab as much of him as possible. The green in his eyes flared brightly.

"Does my hybrid like that?"

"I do," she said, rolling her hips again. "I need more."

He shoved in completely, settling himself as deep as he could go. A full body sigh swept through her. At last. It was perfect. His massive size filled her completely.

"I had no idea," Rhys breathed, his head dropping to bury in her neck. "No idea it could feel so good."

She caressed her hands over his shoulders, down his spine, up to his nape. The short hair of his head prickled against her sensitive fingers, increasing the turmoil of sensations ricocheting throughout her body.

"Me either," she murmured. Never imagined how much pleasure could be found with the right partner. Getting off and making love were two totally different entities.

He pulled his head up again, so she settled her hands upon on his broad back.

"I want to watch you." He pulled almost all the way out, giving her a momentary sense of loss.

Thrusting back in made Alex gasp. All of her nerve endings were dying for more. She wrapped her legs tighter around him and held on as he pulled out and lunged forward. He began a steady pounding rhythm that brought her to the brink of another explosion.

She wanted to hang onto the precipice, afraid she'd never get another moment like this again. Rhys had another idea. He moved his hand between them and found her ultra-sensitive nub again. The first stroke had her jacking her pelvis off the bed, an involuntary cry of pure pleasure escaping her lips.

An expression of unfiltered male satisfaction filled Rhys' handsome face; his pace increased. Alex's vision splintered apart. She yelled, she cried his name, she clawed his back. The whole time, he watched her. The brief seconds her vision cleared, she saw the wonder in his eyes, glimpsed her own reflection.

He had stilled when her orgasm hit, but now as she was coming down from her high, he thrust once. Twice. His own orgasm hit hard and fast. Throwing his head back, he roared her name. His hips quivered as he jerked his release. His warmth spread through her center, and when his arms gave out, she cradled him in her embrace.

They both lay spent. He was still inside her, still hard, but like her, he also settled into the moment. Let their history lie, kept their uncertain future from clouding the moment.

Rhys propped on his elbows to gaze down at her. "That was the most beautiful thing I've ever seen." He kissed her lightly on the lips. "Your eyes get the loveliest burgundy glow within their green depths."

Confused, Alex cocked her head at him. "My eyes glowed red?"

He chuckled softly. "You are part vampire. Hasn't anyone ever noticed?"

Uh, no. "Not since I was a kid. If they had, there would have been some serious questions raised. Besides, as little of me was involved with others as could be helped."

His bent his head to kiss the tip of her nose, an action that made her feel delicate, feminine. "Good. I get all of you."

Yes. She would always be his, even if their moments had to be stolen. She wouldn't let concerns over her future spoil the night. Tonight was for her. For the last twelve years, she got tonight.

Dropping his head again, he licked the rim of her ear causing a delightful shiver to move through her body. "I want to mark you."

She rocked into him, her body already wanting, needing, more of him. He desired to mark her. He wanted her permission. Could she give it?

What if she needed to go on the run? Then she'd smell like she was claimed to other shifters. No big. It's not like she planned to ever be with anyone else again, to use her body as a tool or a weapon. She didn't even want to leave the option out there. No one could predict the future, but one thing was for sure, she wouldn't let herself be used again.

So the question was: What did she want? She wanted to be with Rhys. And if the council won and nothing changed, if she lived without Rhys, she wanted to carry his mark.

To show he had her permission, she unwrapped her legs and pushed him away. His expression was guarded, like he wouldn't show her his disappointment thinking she was refusing his claim.

Her sultry smirk flamed the light in his eyes. He flipped over onto her belly. If he wanted to mark her, then they would do it the way their people had been doing it for centuries. He would also carry her mark before the night was over—because this was only the beginning.

He growled as he caught her hips. With a strong thrust, he buried himself deep. There was no pause as he started a frantic tempo. The closer she got to the orgasm that was building rapidly, the harder she ground back into him.

His hands were digging into her sides, but he released one, almost collapsing on top of her, maintaining his unrelenting pace. She was moaning, panting, the pleasure divine. With one hand bracing the bed, he let go of her waist and wrapped his arm around her middle, holding her while he pounded into her from behind.

Just as her orgasm crested and she cried out, his mouth descended to the junction of her shoulder and neck. The strike of the bite marking her increased the intensity of the orgasm. The cry of his name on her lips turned into a steady, wordless wail.

How could an orgasm have so much power? Her body shook with the force. Sometime during her peak, Rhys found his release, his thrusts slowing as he emptied within her.

His hot mouth disengaged from her, and he leisurely licked along the bite. They both collapsed at the same time, and he pulled out of her. He rolled onto his side and drew her into him.

Putting up no resistance, content for the moment, her need for him temporarily sated, she rested her head on his arm. "For the record, I get to bite you next."

His cock twitched against her. It had been at half-mast until she spoke.

"God, yes."

Chapter Fourteen

Alex was his.
She let him claim her. Then she claimed him.

She was his. He was hers.

Rhys was damn near giddy. After meeting his mate, finding out she worked for the bad guys, then finding out she wasn't evil, then worrying Madame G would kill her, and, worst of all, six months with total radio silence from her, he finally had her. Her body was a paradise. He wanted his mouth on her at all times, he wanted to be buried inside of her any chance he could get. She was addicting, and she was all his.

Oh, he knew, *he knew*, she still planned on taking off if things with the council didn't end satisfactorily. No, she wouldn't be used as a pawn anymore. No longer a weapon at other's discretion. Rhys knew her too well. She would leave before that happened. She would sacrifice herself. Again. Only she didn't know that he wouldn't let her. Wherever she went, he would follow. As much as his duty was to his people, they'd had him for three centuries. It was his turn now. She was his mate. He didn't even mind waiting until after the mess with the council was settled to have a ceremony to make their mating official. As long as he had her, he didn't need a dagger and blood bond to eternally bind them together.

Rhys stretched over her and pushed forward, her body rose to meet his. All night, into the morning, they only paused in their lovemaking for a couple hours of sleep here and there. Right now, he was lazily stroking within her hot, tight channel, while his mouth tasted as much of her skin as possible.

She liked hard and fast and, with her, it was exhilarating. What she really seemed to enjoy were the sessions where they took their time, like they were doing right now. He soaked in the rapture on her face when she came, and he could feel her studying his features, watching his body as he spent himself inside her.

Alex sighed into him, he kept up his slow rhythm. Stroking them both to their peak, their tongues tangling until they crested together, easy ecstasy.

He caught his breath and murmured against her lips. "We should flash and meet the rest,"

"All right."

She gave him a gentle shove. He hated to leave the cocoon of her body.

"I need to shower first." She rolled off the bed and stood up. Before she disappeared into the bathroom, she threw a coy glance over her shoulder. "Are you going to join me?"

Hell. Yes.

During their shower, they scrubbed each other down, and delayed a few more minutes as he took her in a frenzy against the flimsy shower stall until the warm water ran cold. They rinsed off in a hurry and climbed out. Drying off, he tried not watch her knowing it would cause another delay.

The fangs marks in his neck throbbed with an erotic beat that he treasured, knowing they would be fully healed soon. In companionable silence, they each got dressed and checked their weapons.

"Ready?" She held her hand out to flash them to the cabin.

No. He wanted to stay in this cheap, quaint motel room for another week. Maybe two. Never leave the room and order in nothing but pizza and soda.

"Totes." His use of her term made her mouth twitch and her eyes light with humor. He wanted to spend the rest of his life trying to accomplish that…when he wasn't immersed in her lush body.

Rhys took a deep breath to ready himself for the flash and the accompanying feeling that his intestines were trying to climb out of his stomach through his throat. When his hand touched hers, she latched on and the room disappeared.

When Rhys blinked next, he was surrounded by the smell of pine and a subtle scent of lake water. His vision was wonky, his guts twisted, but he sucked in deep breaths until the sensations passed. To help stabilize himself, he concentrated on the logs that made up the wall he was facing.

Alex waited for him to settle before she did anything. He finally nodded. They both cocked their heads, listening for sounds coming through the cabin. He heard amenable conversation and smelled a scent that made his mouth water.

Bacon. A lot of it. It had been *months* since he'd had bacon.

"Yoo-hoo? Ladies, we've arrived!" Alex opened the door and sauntered out from the empty room.

The conversation died as he followed Alex down the hall to the open dining room and kitchen.

"We grabbed extra bacon out of the freezer last night." Malcolm stood next to the table. "Have you eaten yet?"

Alex was already snatching a fistful of bacon off the heaping pile on the counter and handing some to Rhys. It was gone in two seconds, and he reached around her for more.

At the table, Sylva sat rigidly, her eyes downcast, her body language suggesting she was severely uncomfortable in a room full of males. Alex's female presence probably wasn't reassuring since she was strapped with as many weapons as the males and her height put her at least six inches taller than Sylva.

Damon and William flanked her on each side. Rhys guessed they must have become quite protective of the timid shifter during their captivity. The males were rested and fresh, but lines of tension marred their features.

"What now, Boss?" Malcolm crossed his arms and waited for Rhys to finish chewing.

"I'm not your boss anymore." Alex handed him some milk that he sucked down.

Malcolm snorted. "We all know Bennett is acting commander under duress. Dude hasn't quit bitching since you left."

For some reason, that made Rhys feel better. Bennett was a worthy leader, just because he didn't feel ready for the position didn't mean he didn't perform his duties admirably. Would Rhys jump at the chance to get his old post back? Of course. But only if it meant Alex was at his side.

"What does Bennett know?" Alex asked between mouthfuls of bagel.

"Commander Young is insanely difficult to get information to. Dani keeps finding bugs hidden in the damn walls, clogging up our phones. It's ridiculous." Malcolm sneered in disgust while Harrison shook his head. "The newbs Councilman Seether sent to us are quite the spies. The way Master Bellamy rides 'em all day, they should be too sore and tired to lift their arms to plant listening devices."

That was a complication. His Guardian pack was the only one they could trust. Surely there were others out there who weren't corrupt and full of deceit. Time was too critical to find out. For now, it was just them.

"So it's us against the council?" Rhys' mind spun, searching for solutions. Eventually, they would need to get to Bennett. He would be the one to officially launch a complaint and demand an investigation into the council's actions.

"Yeppers."

Alex reclined back against the counter and crossed her feet and arms, looking pointedly at Damon. "But we need to find his Lily first or no one will believe us."

Damon's jaw clenched, his fair hair shadowed his eyes. "I'm not endangering her."

"I get it, I do," she replied. "But what if we aren't the first to get to her?"

He swept his hair off his face, his expression defiant. "What if we fail?" He shook his head. "No. My testimony, or nothing."

Alex narrowed her eyes at him, but Rhys recognized the burgeoning respect their green depths. "Lily is in danger regardless. If we can find her, we can get her to a safe place."

"Which is where?" Damon countered.

The room went silent. Lily could stay with them and be protected by Rhys, Alex, and the twins. They were already guarding and protecting the other three, although Damon and William could fight if needed. Mostly, the three former prisoners needed to be watched and prevented from doing something stupid that would put them all at risk.

"I have an idea, but you might not like it."
Even though Alex was talking to the entire room,
she looked directly at him. "Demetrius Devereux."

She was right. He hated the idea. Biting back a
"fuck no," Rhys forced himself to consider her
suggestion. "Is he solidly established as the leader
for the vampires?" Please say no.

"As much as he can be while some of the old
timers fight against the change in regime. It was a
long time coming, though, and he has solid support
in most of the population."

William shifted in his seat, sensing unease from
his son. "We can't trust Lily with her own kind any
more than we can trust her safety to shifters."

"You can trust her with D." Alex was right.
Rhys grudgingly respected the male. If it hadn't
been for him, Rhys wouldn't have gotten Alex out,
and she wouldn't be here today. The male
orchestrated the revolt against his own council and
was intent on leading his people in the right
direction.

"What if this Demetrius Devereux keeps Lily
away from me?" Damon still held hostility in his
gaze. "Or what if we have kids, then what about
them? They would be hybrids, targets."

"He said he'd expect the same out of hybrids
that he expects out of his vampires." Alex's fingers
tapped rhythmically on her arm.

Rhys watched her fidget. Her nervous energy
offset his calm demeanor.

"That's great for hybrids under his command." Damon was shaking his head. "We know what the current Lycan Council's view on hybrids is. What will the new council's view be?"

Alex tensed next to him. That question had been weighing heavily on her mind, too. Demetrius may have promised her amnesty, but it would do her no good if the shifters didn't do the same. Both species would want her to pick one to side to obey.

William filled in where his son left off. "Will either side be truly content with an individual, much less an entire family, choosing sides?"

Rhys' mind started formulating a plan. A tentative plan, one that might meet with great resistance. From both sides. Or as Alex was proof of, there were now more than two sides.

"We're planning too small scale. We need to think bigger." Rhys got the attention of everyone in the room. "We won't need Lily, but we need to get Demetrius here."

Chapter Fifteen

"**H**oly shit!" Bennett hissed and sat upright at Alex's sudden appearance in his office. "What the hell do you think you're doing?" Before she could speak, he held up a hand and turned on a white noise machine. "Fuckers think they're clever."

Alex smirked at the male's scowl. "Thought I'd drop in for a visit since it's been a few days."

"The council's pissed. Fucking Seether has been breathing down my damn neck." Bennett kept his voice low, but Alex's sensitive ears easily picked out his words. "Did you get Fitzsimmons out?"

"We did. Along with some witnesses we can use to prove the council is hunting my kind. I can explain more, but first you need to come with me."

Bennett's handsome face blanched. "You mean like that flashing shit?"

"Mmm-hmm." She kind of enjoyed his discomfort. Yes, he could be called her nephew since he was mated to Sarah, but that didn't mean it was any less fun to mess with him. "I'm almost sure I can get you back okay."

He gave a curt shake of his head. "Almost sure? What would happen if you couldn't?"

She casually shrugged and lied. "Dunno." Too bad she couldn't stop her wicked grin. "Nah, we'd just get dumped somewhere between here and the lake house."

"That's like five hundred miles away."

"Chill. I just fed from Rhys, so I've got the power."

Bennett held his hand up again. "TMI, dude."

Alex couldn't help but grin again, feeling the surge of Rhys' blood coursing through her veins. "C'mon, Benji. Let Auntie take you on a trip."

The blond scowled hard at her, but finally stood up to come around his desk and grab her hand. "We'll be back soon, right? If Sarah finds out I left without telling her, she's going to not-cuss up a storm at me."

Sarah's aversion to swearing was well known around the lodge. It didn't mean anyone watched their mouth, just that she preferred not to swear herself. Alex figured Bennett did enough for both of them.

"You'll get the pleasure of telling her you left and came back, all without her knowing."

A frown marred Bennett's handsome face. "Damn. I'm not going to win either way."

Alex latched onto the newest member of her family and flashed them back to the lake cabin.

Whoa. As Bennett staggered next to her, her heart beat like a jackhammer. Long distance flashing was only for the powerful vampires. Alex might only be half, but her mother had been a fierce creature in her day. That, combined with Rhys' blood, gave her enough of a boost to transport with a passenger. She'd need to feed again before she brought Bennett back and got stuck at the lodge.

"That sucked," Bennett wheezed.

She slapped him on the back. "You took it like a man. Like a two-hundred and thirty pound shifter male who can't flash worth a damn."

He shot her a dirty look, but a faint smile touched his lips. They might not be besties, but they were getting there.

"Let's go join the party."

He followed her out of the room Alex fondly began to think of as "the flashing chamber." Conversation drifted from the dining room. Mainly from Demetrius, who must have arrived right as she left to get Bennett. The vampire was interrogating Damon about the night his mate, Lily, had been attacked. Damon and his father sat at the table, flanking Sylva. Malcolm and Harrison stood at one end of the dining room, while Rhys stood on the other. Demetrius remained standing, across from the three shifters he was questioning.

Demetrius paused as Alex and Bennett walked into the room. His nostrils flared and his eyes warmed in her direction. "Ah. I thought I smelled your mark on the brooding shifter in the corner. I see you only need to make it official now, love."

Malcolm's eyebrows shot up when he heard Demetrius' endearment. Harrison scowled at the vampire. Both males were extremely loyal to her mate.

"It's official enough," Rhys smoothly replied.

The vampire broke out in a grin, his fangs flashing, and Alex was relieved to see that Rhys no longer seemed to despise the male. They weren't drinking buddies or anything, but the two males were very similar. She thought of Demetrius as a friend and would be glad if Rhys could more than tolerate his presence.

"Don't babysit your mailbox waiting for an invitation to our mating ceremony," she teased.

Demetrius put his hands over his heart. "You wound me." The smile dropped from his face and he was back to business. "Other than helping with this Lily that Damon's been telling me about, what did you drag me here for?"

She had called Demetrius the previous day to persuade him he needed to drive out to the cabin. Flashing would've been faster, but since Demetrius had never been there before, Alex would have to flash with him. If they could convince Demetrius to come to them, she could save her strength to flash to Bennett and bring him to the cabin.

Rhys was the first to speak. "Tell us what your mission is in leading your people."

"Like shifters, vampires need a more modern government. One less concerned about hiding and keeping secrets, and one more concerned about protecting and guiding their people into the future. We're integrating, like it or not." Demetrius nodded toward Damon, his pale-green eyes grim. "The species are mixing. I aim to see that my people survive and incorporate themselves into the human world without spilling our secrets, or getting themselves killed keeping them."

"What about hybrids?"

Demetrius shrugged his powerful shoulders. "Don't care. They'll need to follow the same rules."

"That sounds amazing," William spoke, his tone sounding like he had just heard a fairy tale. "Shifters need the same out of their government. But I fail to see how either council can adequately protect any of my future grandchildren, which will be hybrids."

"If they follow me, I'll protect them," Demetrius said, arrogantly.

"Why do they need to choose sides?" Rhys stepped forward, he had everyone's attention. "Our species are at the point where our paths are converging. Our governments should converge with it."

Malcolm's eyes went wide. "Are you talking about blending the councils?" Alex knew the twins had grown up with their councilman father. This train of thought was way outside of the box for them.

Demetrius' gaze was speculative. "Do you think any seats on your current council would be willing to work with me?"

"Hybrids still wouldn't have representation," Damon pointed out. "But it sounds better than two separate entities trying to govern populations that exists side-by-side."

"A hybrid would sit on the council," Demetrius suggested, his eyes lifting to her. "Are you up for the job?"

"Fuck no." Alex didn't even have to think about that. "I'm not a politician." She smiled. "But maybe I know someone who would be good for the job."

Rhys didn't ask who she was thinking of. The population of hybrids was small. He would figure it out. "We need to sit and figure out how a new government would work, then show up tomorrow before the council convenes."

"Then why am I here?" Bennett was still standing with Alex in the doorway. He'd been so still she almost forgot he was there.

Rhys' eyes gleamed. "As commander of one of the Guardian packs, only you can launch a formal complaint against the council itself. One severe enough, it calls for the immediate execution of all members involved."

Bennett's dark-blue eyes brightened with mirth. "I'll bet those old bastards forgot that little tidbit when they ordered the murders of their own people." He looked at the twins. "How are you two doing with this?"

Harrison dropped his eyes, while Malcolm met Bennett's gaze unflinchingly. "Our father isn't involved."

"What if he is?" Bennett pushed.

"He isn't. But if he admits to ordering the murders of women, children, and innocent shifters, then he needs to face his punishment."

Sylva cleared her throat. "That's all well and good. You can lead your people into the future. Does the future include making laws that clan leaders can't force their daughters to mate? Does the future include making colonies that keep themselves isolated in order to preserve their own internal power face the light? Will the shifters born into isolation be able not to just grow up hearing rumors of a world where we're free to make our own decisions, but actually experience it?"

It was the most any of them had heard her speak. The female's violet eyes lit with more fire, the more she talked. Demetrius cocked his head at her, as if waiting to hear more.

Emboldened, she continued. "If we can overthrow our own government, we need to dive into the issues that enabled the leaders to gain so much power in the first place. Isolated colonies need education, they need a form of leadership that isn't just by birthright or might." Her tone dripped with bitterness. "All of our people need this change." Her voice caught and her gaze flicked up to Alex. "Not just hybrids."

Alex could see the enormity of what Sylva said sink in with the rest of the Guardians. They all knew how many colonies were squirreled away, deep in the woods and forests. They barely blended when forced to, but some clans were very selective on who they let mingle with humans. Even when Alex had to go deal with Madame G's shifter spies, she saw the toll it took on some inhabitants. Stuck in unhappy matings, not allowed to roam the world and meet their destined love, or even just live freely. Eventually, the lack of a solid mating bond drives a shifter to go feral, crazy. The lack of outside contact, or expression of themselves, was making them go rogue and break away from their own society. Alex had dealt with enough of both of those in her short time.

It occurred to her that she was probably considered a rogue. A shifter who didn't follow the rules. The irony that a Guardian was her mate wasn't lost on her. If overthrowing the council didn't work, could she live without Rhys and stay sane? She knew what it was like in his arms. Could she walk away from him so he could do his job?

Bennett ran a hand through his always messed-up hair and blew out a gusty breath. "Y'all, we'd better get started planning before Sarah goes looking for me."

***

Things didn't move as quickly as projected. Getting plans made, getting people in place, even getting hold of some of the individuals, took time. Especially when half of those involved couldn't flash, but had to drive. Bennett was driving from West Creek to the council's hearing, and the twins were bringing the three former prisoners.

Rhys was waiting at the cabin with Alex, who was sipping her coffee and checking the time.

"Bennett's appointment with the council begins in fifteen minutes," she said.

"Good. We should get going." He snagged her mug and took a drink, wrinkling his nose as he set it on the counter. He'd never get used to the stuff.

Alex made to grab his hand and flash.

"Wait."

She stopped, her hand hovering above his arm, and waited for him to continue.

"Whatever happens, we stay together."

A fleeting look of regret crossed her face. "Rhys, your pack will need you."

He firmly shook his head. "They've been doing just fine without me for six months. You are my life. Where you go, I go."

She had that look. The one where she was deciding whether she would takeoff, or whether she'd tell him first and find a way to leave without him.

"Where you go, I go," he stressed.

"If Councilman Seether and Hargrath remain in power, I can't stay."

"Honey," he grabbed her and pulled her in close, "if they stay in power, my entire pack will be in trouble anyway. It'd be best if we all disappeared. If this does work, though, and I go back to being Commander Fitzsimmons? You and me. Together."

Her hands skated up his chest and snaked them around his neck. "I'll have to decide what I'm going to be when I grow up."

That one caught Rhys off guard. "I thought you'd want to become a Guardian?"

"And work for you?" she teased, then her vibrant eyes turned serious. "I never wanted to be a fighter." Her tone was solemn. "It became a part of who I am, but it's not what I want to do forever. I've been too busy surviving to think there was anything else for me. I'd been certain that I couldn't stay with you and would have to go on the run."

"Then we need to make sure you have time to decide what you want to do with your life. Just know that I can't do my job and let you go. If I go back to being Commander Fitzsimmons, it will only be because we have new leadership that allows me to have a hybrid mate. Let's go." He gave her a chaste kiss on the forehead. Anything more and he'd delay them too long.

Everything went black in a blink as Alex flashed him to the storage closet next to the room he had his beatings. It was close to the chambers the council held their sessions in, where Bennett should be at that moment.

We're in place, he informed Bennett, after his head quit spinning. Alex stepped away to listen at the door.

I haven't been called in yet. Mercury told the guards he was coming in with me, in less nice terms. I had Jace and Kaitlyn hang back at the lodge, just in case.

Good. If things went south, their loved ones would be protected until they put Plan B into motion, which was to get the hell out of there.

Our ETA is two minutes. Malcolm's voice floated through Rhys' head.

Perfect. It was Bennett this time. *They just gave me the signal to go in front of the council. Malcolm, there's one guard to take your car, and another right inside the door.*

We'll take care of 'em, Malcolm replied.

Alex and I are heading your way, Bennett.

Two guards flank the chamber's doors, Bennett informed him.

Got it.

Alex pulled open the door. "Clear."

He followed her out. Between the two of them, they should have no problem getting to the council's main chambers. He had faced his own tribunal there after they had taken him into custody all those months ago. Alex still had the schematics of the facility committed in her brain.

Timing would be a huge key to their success, otherwise the council's pack of Guardians might be able to detain them.

From Malcolm's report, and Rhys' own observation, the Guardian pack protecting the facility and council members numbered at twenty. When he and Alex were breaking out Damon, his father, and Sylva, he had encountered two of them, other than Mastiff. They were good. But thanks to Master Bellamy, his pack was better. And they had Alex.

She walked confidently next to him. Her black hair was slicked down and tucked behind her ear. "To better fight Guardians with, my pretty," she had told him earlier that morning. They each had a dart gun in hand. They'd win no trust from their people slaughtering indiscriminately. They'd give the council's pack of Guardians a fair hearing before condemning them.

Five guards in the chamber itself, Mercury informed them. Bennett must be busy talking.

"Hey!" a voice shouted behind them.

Alex snapped her fingers. "You know what, sweetheart. I think we went the wrong way. Perhaps we should ask for directions."

"Identify yourselves," a female voice demanded from back down the hallway.

Alex put her hand on her hip. "I think we're lost," she called back over her shoulder. "We're supposed to get mated by the council this afternoon."

Rhys heard the two Guardians behind them move like they were drawing weapons. He spun at the same time Alex did, their own guns raised, and they fired simultaneously. Each guard was hit with a red-tipped dart. It wouldn't knock them out instantly, so both Rhys and Alex lunged for the pair, diving to dodge the impending bullets.

The female fired a shot before she stumbled, the tranquilizer quickly taking effect. The male was already slumping against the wall, dropping his gun as he slid to the floor. The gun clambered to the floor and went off.

Rhys flinched, hoping a ricochet didn't get him in the head. Alex slid, nabbed the female guard's weapon and deftly caught her body before the Guardian slammed face first onto the hard floor.

"You hit?" Rhys asked in the sudden silence. He did a quick assessment of himself when he stood, then went to the fallen male Guardian.

Alex was already up and patting down the female, ridding her of any other weapons, which were considerably less than Rhys' own Guardians carried.

"Just a graze." She deposited her cache by the wall and dragged the unconscious guard to the room where Rhys had spent many interrogations.

Rhys stopped what he was doing to assess his mate. "Just a graze" to Alex could be anything. She didn't seem slowed in the slightest as she dumped her load in the room and held the door open for Rhys to do the same.

She cocked an eyebrow at him. "Just because we're having sex doesn't mean I've gone all soft in the field."

"I know." He picked up the male, hauled him to the room, and dumped him next to the female. He turned to face her. "But I worry about you because I love you."

She blinked at his confession, then smiled. "Loving a hot dude doesn't make me any less of a bad ass."

He grinned like fool. Of course, they'd been in love with each other forever, but to be at a point where they could profess it…amazing. Too bad he couldn't bask in the glow.

They both took off down the hall, steadily making their way to the main chamber. Malcolm had told them that when the council was holding a session, most of the facility's staff sat in to watch. It was an easy get-out-of-work-free card.

Rhys switched to mental communication. *We're right around the corner from the chamber's entrance. Malcolm?*

Boss.

Ready?

It's on.

Rhys turned his mind speak toward Bennett. *It's time.*

With everyone ready, Rhys and Alex turned into the main chamber, dart guns raised. The entrance appeared unmanned, but Rhys smelled two males.

From each side, two shifters lunged for them. The Guardians must have either sensed them approaching or the two Rhys and Alex had encountered had gotten off a mental warning before passing out. Then there was the highly inconvenient gunfire.

Rhys threw an elbow out at the shifter attacking him, while using his other arm to bring down the butt of his gun on the male's head. His elbow was deflected, but Rhys heard a satisfying grunt from his other hit. The male bent down, shoving a shoulder into Rhys' gut, so Rhys brought up a knee once, twice. The Guardian got his arms around Rhys and tried to throw him into the wall. Rhys kept pounding the butt of his gun into the male.

His back hit the wall. An "oomph" was cut off when Rhys' head jerked back and hit the solid surface. He shook off the pain shooting through his skull as he was dragged forward again, and turned the barrel of his gun into the male's ribs. Rhys flew back with even more force than before, so he pulled the trigger and braced himself.

Thudding back into the wall, he kept from slamming his head again and brought his knee up to the male's ribs. The arms around his torso loosened. The guard fell to his hands and knees. Rhys kicked him in the ribs to keep the male from pulling any weapons at the last minute. The downed male fell over onto his side, his eyes closed and head lolling.

Thank Doc and his home brew tranquilizers.

Alex had already subdued the Guardian who had attacked her. He was pressed face first into the floor with her knee in his back. A red dart stuck out of his shoulder. Alex held him down until the tranq took effect.

Both Rhys and Alex were reloading their dart guns when Rhys detected a familiar scent. He spun just in time to see the large blond Guardian who had given him more pain than anyone in his life come flying around the corner.

Rhys met Mastiff head on, both males diving at each other with fists flying.

Mastiff's size was almost a drawback. He pulled back a beefy fist, but Rhys let a left hook and right hook fly, before the male could even finish his move.

"It's different when your victim isn't chained down." Rhys taunted the male through gritted teeth.

Mastiff shook off the hits and kicked out. Rhys danced out of the way and used the advantage of his speed to come back at Mastiff. He grabbed the male's head and slammed it down as he was bringing his knee up. The blow to Mastiff's head disorientated him, making him slow. Rhys kept whaling on him. Fists, knees, boots to the shins. Whatever it took to drop the massive Guardian.

With a roar, Mastiff pushed Rhys back and rose to his full height, which was a good four inches taller than Rhys. Rhys didn't waste any time. If he got hit with one of the male's beefy mallets, it would slow him down too much and give Mastiff an advantage.

Rhys went at the male like a freight train, slamming him into the wall, while he pummeled the male's body. Mastiff used his size to get an arm around Rhys and spin him, locking him in a choke hold.

Now that Rhys was turned around, he could see that Malcolm and Harrison had made it into the building. Damon and William were watching over Sylva, warily eyeing Mastiff in case he came for them next.

The twins and Alex were trying to break into the locked chamber. They were using anything that wasn't bolted down to hit the sturdy wooden doors.

And didn't that give Rhys an idea. He was losing air. Mastiff's hold was unrelenting. Rhys' face grew hot, was probably changing colors. He let his weight give a little, let Mastiff think he was winning.

Away. From. The door. Rhys' mental commands were hitched. He needed to act. Now.

The path to the door cleared. Before his strength drained away with his oxygen supply, he grabbed onto Mastiff's arms. The male probably thought it was to try to pry him off. Instead, Rhys held tight and used every scrap of power he had left to lunge toward the door.

The strategy caught Mastiff off guard. It was perfect timing. Rhys dragged Mastiff ahead, and just as the male was going to put up resistance,

Rhys switched tactics. With the door five feet away, he doubled over and twisted. The move sent Mastiff flying over Rhys' head. The male's chokehold held Rhys firmly, so both males went flying into the doors, but Rhys was protected by Mastiff's larger frame.

The sounds of wood groaning and splintering as the doors broke apart under the assault, filled the stunned chamber.

Tumbling through the opening, Mastiff finally released him when the male's head hit the floor of the chamber with a resounding crack. Rhys landed on top of the unconscious goliath and rolled off, gasping in lungfuls of air.

The rest of the shifters and Alex came pouring in after him, guns raised. Only this time, all the guns used bullets, not darts. Rhys drew his own 9mm, and before he could turn to assess the situation, all hell broke loose.

The five council Guardians in the chamber had been holding Bennett and Mercury at gunpoint, but had turned at the sound of Mastiff being thrown through the door. When Alex and the others entered, it provided Bennett and Mercury the opening they needed.

Bennett dived for the Guardian in front of him, while Mercury lunged to right. To add to the chaos, Mercury sent a buffet of wind though the chambers to disorient everyone. It was part of the plan and the twins and Alex were prepared. Damon and William were also prepared, but from their gaping mouths and darting gazes, Mercury's talent of manipulating wind unnerved them. Sylva cowered in the doorway, tentatively holding her gun, glaring at the unconscious Mastiff, who Rhys stood over.

Gunshots echoed through the chamber. The staff, there to observe the proceedings, were screaming and cowering beneath their seats. Three of the council members were sneaking out the back exit. Rhys wanted to go after them, but a council Guardian was trying to sneak up behind him.

The burn of a bullet tore through his shoulder.

Bastard. He spun on the male, who had already fired off another shot. The bullet lodged into his thigh. He didn't want to shoot indiscriminately in the chamber, but he didn't have time anyway. The other Guardian was on him.

Rhys might be worn out from his battle with Mastiff, but the male was no match for him. He kicked the male's feet out from under him, and shot him on his way down. Then he slammed his fist into the male's face, hard enough to knock him out.

Probing his injured shoulder with his good hand, he was glad to find it wasn't serious. His leg was on fire, but nothing major was hit and the injury could wait. When Rhys turned to find where he was needed next, he saw the other four council Guardians were already subdued. The chamber had fallen quiet.

A lone gun blast rang through the air and Rhys tensed, waiting to see what, or who, had been hit. A staffer screamed. Rhys followed her horrified gaze.

There Mastiff lay, in a different position than Rhys had left him, a wicked knife in the male's hand. A red bloom streamed from his forehead.

Rhys raised his gaze to Sylva still holding her gun, aiming it at Mastiff. She noticed everyone looking at her and hesitantly lowered it. It wasn't a silver bullet, but it'd keep the giant down for a long while.

"He was going for you." Her violet eyes were defiant. "M-my mother taught me how to shoot. Just like she taught me how to take care of my heartless mate."

"Didn't see that coming," Alex muttered.

The group of staffers who were huddled in the chamber started murmuring. The council members who had tried leaving through the back exit were marched back in, their arms raised. Behind them stalked E with a shotgun trained on them.

Rhys grinned, but Alex's smile was bigger. "Biggie, you stud, you."

Finding the former Agent hadn't been easy. He'd chucked the burner phone, but left enough bread crumbs for Bennett to track him down. Once E heard their plan, and their job for him, he was fully on board and glad for the possibility to bring his family home.

"Call the rest of your Guardians off," Rhys demanded to the council members.

They all glared at him defiantly, except for Wallace. "Done."

Seether gasped, outraged, and glared at his fellow council member.

Wallace rolled his eyes. "Old man, this has been a long time coming. This," the twin's father gestured around him, "is what happens when you try to fill the role of deity for the people you're governing."

"As I was saying before the interruption," Bennett said, smoothly, "my pack is calling for the dissolution of the Lycan Council, citing crimes against its own people."

Councilman Seether was shaking. "You have no proof."

"Oh, but I do." A smooth voice chimed in from the doorway. "I've gotten names from questioning *former* vampire leaders. I've got a vampire and her shifter mate who were targeted by the council's Guardians, and…" Demetrius stepped gracefully over the debris in the doorway. He was flanked by the former Agents R and Z. He gave a sidelong glance to Rhys. "I have a dream walker who has dream-witnessed several accounts where Seether and Hargrath ordered assassinations of their own people."

Both Seether and Hargrath paled before turning red with rage. Wallace didn't look one bit surprised, but maybe a little smug that the two older members were finally busted. The two younger council members, Demke and Ute, appeared completely taken aback by the accusations.

"It's a new age," Bennett announced. "So this is how it's gonna go. We've designed a new government. One formed of all the different species. Well, except for humans."

Seether and Hargrath turned their dark gazes on Alex. She stared back defiantly.

"You think our people will be led by her?" Hargrath sneered.

"As opposed to being killed by you?" she asked in a sugary sweet voice. "For the good of the people?"

"This is how we're going to do it, ladies and gents." Demetrius strode up to the dais and arrogantly turned his back on the council members. Former council members. "Representing Team Vampire is myself and my trusted friend, Zohana Chevalier." He held his hand out to present the tall female vampire who had arrived with him.

Rhys saw Alex mouth to E. *She's still a Zitch.*

E ruefully shook his head.

"Representing Team Hybrid, is the one and only," Demetrius paused for dramatic effect and everyone turned to stare at Alex, "John King." Alex smirked back at the surprised crowd.

On cue, a tall, fair-haired male strode into the room. His facial features looked remarkably like his sister's and he had the same bright, cunning eyes.

The male's nostril's flared and his eyes scanned the room, until they landed on Bennett and narrowed. The males gave each other a small, assessing nod. It was the first time Bennett had met his mate's father.

"We'll add representation as their population grows. As for Team Shifter," Demetrius continued, "we'll have to hold two slots until the lot of you can decide on your new leaders."

A disgruntled Hargrath lunged up to the dais, the glint of a blade flashing in his hand. Gasps escaped the staffers, but Demetrius didn't twitch.

Before the male reached Demetrius, Agent R appeared behind him. He grabbed Hargrath, yanked him back, and took him down to the floor. With a flash of fang, R bent over the male and sank in deep. Rhys heard, more than saw, the messy conclusion to the councilman.

"Thank you, Rourke." The fresh scent of metallic blood saturated the air. Demetrius' nostrils flared, his eyes reflected red. "Anyone else have anything to say?" He scanned the room. "Now then. Shall we proceed with the discussion?"

Epilogue

Two weeks later...

Alex came back from her four-legged run in the woods and padded up the stairs to the door. She flowed back into her human form and headed straight for the shower.

Her morning runs were becoming her favorite part of the day. Sometimes, she ran her wolf, sometimes she ran with Cassie Stockwell. It was nice to run with Cassie as a friend, and not because the shrink was her target.

She and Rhys had spent two days at the old council's facility helping plan and set the new ruling body in place. Only one of the previous council's members was allowed to stay, Demke. Rhys and Demetrius figured it would be an easier transition for shifters if they kept him. Sylva's diatribe at the cabin, and aid in shooting Mastiff, earned her the remaining shifter slot. The female had more steel in her than anyone had originally thought. Alex predicted Sylva would become the most outspoken one on the council, heralding a change for the way isolated shifter colonies conducted their business.

Alex's brother, John, seemed comfortable with his new role. When Alex had flashed to his doorstep to tell him about their plan with the new government, he had readily agreed to help lead. He and Kenna could finally live a life out in the open, and see their children as often as they wanted. In fact, her brother and his wife had been staying at the lodge for a few days and would be leaving soon.

The new council—they hadn't decided yet on an official name—put Seether in prison, along with the pack of Guardians who served the former council. They had decided to wait on trials until they dealt with getting the new government accepted by shifters and vampires alike.

Her shower done, Alex was drying off when Rhys' voice drifted through her mind.

What are you doing?

A smile touched her face. Bennett had readily freed himself of the commander title and Commander Fitzsimmons was back to overseeing the West Creek Guardians. There was even talk of incorporating vampires into each Guardian pack. It'd be a pretty radical change, but that was the direction they were heading.

Lonely? she purred back.

Absolutely.

She flung her towel over the curtain rod and flashed into Rhys' office.

He was leaning back in his chair with his hands behind his head. When he saw she was completely naked, his eyes burned into her skin. He rose from his chair to prowl around his desk toward her.

He stopped a breath away. She peered up at him through her lashes. "We're getting officially mated in a few hours."

"I know," he growled.

"Are you sure you don't want to wait for tonight?" She knew the answer. They had both missed a lot of time together, and he never passed up an opportunity to be nestled deep inside of her.

"I just need to take the edge off."

"You took the edge off last night. And then this morning." She was undoing his pants as he backed her into the wall.

"Those were just to keep me sane."

She looked up at him and bit her lip, flashing him a little fang. His pupils dilated and he sucked in a breath. Grabbing onto him, she whipped them both around, so his back was against the wall. Sinking down to her knees, she pulled his length free.

He watched her, his hands lovingly running through her hair. "I love seeing you like this. I love your body. I just fucking love you."

He also never failed to profess his love. She couldn't get sappy no matter how hard she tried. The closest she got was during their long, lovemaking sessions was when she moaned her love for him as he made her come over and over. She was pretty sure he preferred that over poetry anyway.

She held his gaze as she took him into her mouth.

***

Alex perused the books on Rhys' shelf. Their shelf. She had to start thinking of this cabin as hers. After tonight, it would be official, and their mating bond would be complete. She was looking forward to it. She really was. Her family and all of Rhys' pack would be there.

Her insides still hummed after her visit to Rhys' office. Even after today, she couldn't wait until tonight when she could be submerged in her mate's existence. The night of the mating ceremony was rumored to be legendary.

But then there was tomorrow. And the day after that, and the day after that.

What the fuck was she going to do with herself? Yes, she loved her morning runs, she loved being with Rhys, she loved becoming a part of his pack and hanging out with her own family. After her period of self-discovery, the awkwardness was gone and she was comfortable with getting to know her loved ones again.

Alex was surrounded by everything she loved, all the good things in life, there was just nothing for her to do. For so long, she thought there was nothing in the world for her but violence. Now she had everything. Everything. But a part of her felt…empty. Unfulfilled.

Sighing, she pulled a book off the shelf. It was a beautiful day, maybe she'd read outside. She would find no answers pacing inside the cabin.

It wasn't long after Alex moved out to the porch to read when she felt a presence. "If you're trying to sneak up on me, you're not doing very well."

She heard a frustrated sigh and Julio came out from behind a tree.

"How does everyone know when I'm close by?" His serious brown eyes, so much like his dad's, held a heavy amount of frustration.

"Because you move like a freight train," she answered with a smile in her voice. Tossing her book down, she trotted down the porch toward him. "You need to become one with your surroundings. Make your movements a part of them, flow with your environment."

Julio was a rapt pupil and a quick study. Alex figured they must've worked for an hour, creeping around the cabin. She taught him how to move silently in his environment. He wasn't close to being tired, but he was getting antsy, wanting to move onto something else. Then he spotted her book, lying on the porch floor by the chair she had been reading in.

"Whatcha reading?"

"Here." She climbed the stairs and tossed it down to him. "Take a look."

Julio grabbed the book and sat on the bottom stair. His mouth moved as he read over the title.

"Monte," Alex helped him out with one of the words.

"*The Count of Monte Cristo*," Julio echoed. "Is it any good?"

Alex shrugged, sitting next to him. "If you like that sort of thing. Why don't you try it?" It can't be any more violent than what Julio went through when he was captured by Madame G. The book wasn't even Alex's, but she knew Rhys wouldn't mind.

His face lit up. "That'd be great. It's been kind of boring." He looked down at his shoes. "I miss school."

Alex could empathize. Not with the school bit, though she had loved school. His whole life had turned around on him too, and he was left wondering what was next. Just like her.

"Mom's going to get some home-schooling courses, but right now she's busy in the lab with Doc." His shoulders lifted and dropped. "I guess, it's better than nothing."

Looking at young Julio, Parrish ran through Alex's mind. Had Parrish gotten any education during his time at Sigma? Maybe his mother taught him what she could, but beyond that?

Then there was baby Dante, who was growing up and would have twin siblings soon. Dani was ecstatic, and terrified. She had expressed her thoughts about how she would keep up as security for the pack with the babies *and* entertain Dante. The woman wanted to be with her kids, but didn't want to leave the pack hanging; she loved her job.

An idea formed in Alex's mind.

***

All of their family and pack members were looking up at her and Rhys on the porch. She was dressed in a simple white gown that almost reached her bare feet, with no other adornments. Rhys wore loose slacks and a plain white shirt. Their clothes were designed to be discarded quickly after their mating ceremony was done. Which was two minutes ago. Before she and Rhys sneaked off, they had made a proposal to the rest of the pack.

"So what do you think?" Alex faced the group.

Her heart pounded. She normally didn't care what people thought, but this was her future. Her future and the future of the pack. Without proper care and training for the kids, what advantage did their pack have?

She glanced down at Dani, relief swamped through the young mother from head to toe. Dante squealed and clapped, and Mercury looked from his son up to Alex. It was like the boy was giving his approval.

Wasn't someone going to say *something*?

"Can she, Mom?" Julio pleaded with Ana, his brow drawn up in hope. Ana smiled at him and looked to E, who shrugged and nodded. Ana's eyes were bright with excitement as she, too, nodded to Alex.

"Do you even like kids?" Mercury asked with his legendary bluntness.

"I fucking love kids, Goldie." Why hadn't she thought of calling the silver-highlighted male that before? It was perfect.

Sarah let out a girly squeak, jumping up and down. The female grabbed Bennett's hand. "Won't that be cool? When we have kids, Aunt Allie will be their teacher!"

Bennett appeared stunned at the thought of having kids, and even more so of Alex being their educator.

Alex glanced up into her mate's eyes. No one had refused outright so he elaborated. "We'd setup a couple of rooms in the lodge as a classroom and a playroom. Any bigger kids, right now it's just Julio, will split their time with her and Master Bellamy. Alex will start working with the little ones, developing any powers that are being expressed and teaching them how to defend themselves, beyond all the normal math and reading."

Parrish's hands moved in communication. Alex had just started studying sign language, but could only pick out a few words.

Master Bellamy, still standing on the porch with them since he had presided over their ceremony, filled her in. "He wants to know if you'll order in some coursework so he can catch up to other shifters his age?"

She stared Parrish directly in his pale-blue eyes. "I'll get you *past* other shifters *twice* your age."

The relieved young male grinned.

"Before Alex and I step away," Rhys gave her a searing once over before turning back to face the crowd, "and you all go celebrate our mating, I want to finalize this plan. Is anyone opposed to Alex overseeing the childcare and education of our pack's young?"

Alex's heart pounded, but she was greeted with complete silence.

"All right then," Rhys drawled, and pulled her in to snake an arm around her waist. "She doesn't start until next week. I want plenty of time with her." He leaned down to whisper in her ear. "I'm going to pick you up and carry you into the cabin in front of everyone, so don't hit me."

He swooped her up and headed toward his front door. The crowd cheered their departure and Alex high-fived Master Bellamy as Rhys carried her past him.

It made sense, Alex realized, why they were all so accepting of her offer to become a teacher to their young. This was a pack of shifters and non-shifters. At one point, they all had faced finding their place in life, and in the pack. Alex could help them do that, she could help their kids do that, and in return, they would help her find her place in the pack, too.

Thank you so much for reading. I'd love to hear what you think. Please consider leaving a review at the retailor the book was purchased from.
~Marie

About the Author

Marie Johnston lives in the upper-Midwest with her husband, four kids, and an old cat. Deciding to trade in her lab coat for a laptop, she's writing down all the tales she's been making up in her head for years. An avid reader of paranormal romance, these are the stories hanging out and waiting to be told, between the demands of work, home, and the endless chauffeuring that comes with children.

For short stories and new information, sign up for my quarterly newsletter at:
www.mariejohnstonwriter.com

Like my Facebook page: Marie Johnston Writer

Follow me on Twitter @mjohnstonwriter

Also by Marie Johnston

The Sigma Menace:
Fever Claim (Book 1)
Primal Claim (Book 2)
True Claim (Book 3)
Reclaim (Book 3.5)
Lawful Claim (Book 4)
Pure Claim (Book 5)

New Vampire Disorder:
Demetrius (Book 1)
Rourke (Book 2)

Pale Moonlight
Birthright (Book 1)

Demetrius
Book one, New Vampire Disorder

*As if overthrowing the vampire government and
helping implement a new council to make vampires,
shifters, and hybrids play nice wasn't enough,
Demetrius Devereux finds a bigger problem to deal
with in an innocent, stubborn, and privileged
beauty.*

*Callista Augustus is the over-protected
daughter of a once-powerful vampire leader.
Discovering her desperate father has tapped into a
well of pure evil, Calli swallows her sense of
betrayal and turns him in. She almost regrets it
when she meets the infamous and arrogant
Demetrius. Forcing herself to work with the male
who ruined her family, Calli's only concern is
saving her father.*

*When Demetrius gets past the infuriating
personality of the righteous female, he realizes
Calli's the one in great danger. He gives her his
help out of duty, until it becomes clear that if he
loses her, he loses everything.*

I'm not done writing about the West Creek shifters!

Birthright
Book One, Pale Moonlight

Porter Denlan's home is in turmoil, his pack lives in fear of their cruel leader, but he knows one female whose birthright can govern them without question. Unfortunately, his nemesis is also searching for her—and it isn't to bring her back to the home she was taken from.

Raised as a human, Maggie Miller wishes she could connect with her species. But when a sexy carpenter makes outrageous claims about her destiny, she blows him off—despite her intense attraction toward the rugged male. Hours after she watched his admirable backside walk out, three brutes attack her. Unable to stay away from her, Porter jumps to her aid; they barely escape.

On the run, they learn what Maggie's birthright truly is—and how it could tear them apart.

Made in the USA
Middletown, DE
21 April 2020